ROOK

ROOK

Blaine C. Readler

FULL ARC PRESS

ROOK

This is a work of fiction. Names, characters, places and incidents are either the product of the author's wild imagination or are used fictitiously. Any resemblance to actual events, locales, organizations, or persons, living, dead, or one foot in the grave, although inevitable and in a weird way complimentary to the author, since it shows he is not so insulated from reality that the products of his imagination are totally alien to the average mind, is nevertheless entirely coincidental and beyond the intent of either the author or the publisher.

Visit us at: http://www.readler.com

E-mail: blaine@readler.com

ISBN: 978-0-9992296-4-4

Printed in the United States of America

I dedicate this book to my honey, as I have dedicated my heart.

ACKNOWLEDGEMENTS

A heartfelt thanks to MTB for her endless stamina in purging inexcusable foibles.

A huzza thanks to James Ward for yet again rendering visually, a hazy idea of a tale.
https://www.jameswardillustrations.com

You can never find the truth. It lies
somewhere between left and right, top and bottom, and
the closer you look, the finer the resolution of cracks that
it falls into. Moral imperative, however, requires that you
search.

—Julius Falschung

Chapter 1

Rook paused, holding his breath as he studied the ground. The cougar tracks were fresh, and so were the intermingled deer tracks. At least that's what Rook decided, even though a little blossom fuzz, fallen from a scratch-baby bush, lay only inside the hoof imprints of the deer. That was probably just a coincidence. The cougar's tracks overlay those of the deer. The cougar was stalking it. Neither animal, predator nor prey, were moving very fast. The deer had not yet sensed its demise.

He looked up and scanned the near distance, listening. No hint yet of the drama about to unfold. The cougar would be totally focused on the deer, no reason to fear what lay behind, after all.

Rook bit his lip. Should he change that? *Could* he change that? The common ritual across all families of the tribe, passed on, ancestor to ancestor since the beginning of time, was that the boy who left the campfire to seek transition could return as a man only if he brought along the paws of a cousin-hunter that he had killed—wolf, bear, or cougar—the three tribes that competed with men for prey. And the "prey," of course, could be any one of them.

The ritual was mostly symbolic. Besting a cousin-hunter was a metaphor for overcoming dependence on the family. The reality was significantly tamer, and useful. Rook could return with a deer or a young moose, and the transition celebration would begin enthusiastically. A stomach full of meat was stiff competition for the abstraction of a metaphor.

That's not to say that full ritual fulfillment was not possible. Rook's great uncle, Beorn, had returned with four wolf paws, and, as told, his feat was the highlight of that year's Great Gathering. Whispered rumors that Beorn had come across a wounded wolf abandoned by his own pack were shushed and ignored. The fact that people were willing to overlook a possible lie, the ultimate insult to Maker, spoke of the power of ritual fulfillment.

This year's Great Gathering in the Valley of Three Rivers was less than two new moons away. His heart thumped a little faster when he thought of it. Suna hadn't promised herself at last year's Gathering—in fact, she hadn't even shown any specific favor towards him. But she hadn't rejected his advances either. That in itself was an invitation to vie for her. He had to achieve transition, of course, before asking Tawnkin, Suna's family leader, for permission. Only men could marry. Family leader permission was another ritual with foregone conclusion, mostly for the sake of tribal unity. When, permission was withheld, it was usually the result of a grudge between family leaders, not because the suitor was unacceptable.

Tawnkin would give his blessing if Rook returned to his family unit with a deer. Suna would look at him with keen interest if he came back with cougar paws.

Rook decided it wouldn't hurt to follow the tracks and see what developed. He hefted his spear over his shoulder and walked on.

The tracks followed a seasonal stream uphill for a while, and then the cougar veered away, off to the right. Rook had accepted by now that the deer's tracks were not actually fresh, at least not concurrent with the cougar, who may have come to the same conclusion. He looked at the cougar's prints loping their way up the scrabbly slope, and headed off after them. He wasn't about to take on a cougar not distracted with stalking, but it was always good to know the habits and travels of a cousin-hunter, even here, a day beyond the edge of the family group hunting range.

Before long, it became difficult to follow the cougar tracks, as loose dirt gave way to bare rock on the rising slope. He was so intent on searching for telltale signs that he stopped short, surprised, when suddenly there, not fifty paces ahead were two cougar cubs watching him intently from the safety of a ledge topping a fall of large boulders. Rook froze. His heart seemed to stop. He couldn't see the opening, but the cougar's lair must be up there somewhere among the rock jumble.

And where there was a lair and two cubs, the mother wouldn't be far away.

He turned, wondering if he should run or slink away, and then gasped. The cougar crouched watching him, two leaps away. She opened her mouth and growled, revealing gleaming sharp dagger teeth.

She hadn't pounced him from behind, probably deciding whether he was a man. Cougars take human children as prey, but they don't willingly go against a man's spear. This was understood, repeated often enough by elders that Rook didn't question whether it was a myth. He held his breath as he lifted the spear slowly off his shoulder, expecting a lunge and slashing claws at any moment.

To lie, whether to another human or to an animal, was a grave offense in the eyes of Maker. Terror clutched at his gut, though, and, in any case, he was on the cusp. This was essentially a paradox—besting a cougar was in itself entry to manhood.

"I am a man!" Rook called, and the cougar's head edged back at the outburst.

Allowing himself a sliver of hope and keeping the spear between his throat and the cougar, Rook slowly edged sideways, making for a side exit down the slope. The cougar's eyes narrowed, and she sprang to the side, blocking him.

She knows I lied, he thought. To satisfy Maker—to restore balance—she must now kill him. His mind raced. There was no way out. *Maybe*, he thought, willing the idea to be true, *if I kill her, and save the cubs, Maker will be mollified*. It didn't really make sense, but such is the logic of desperation.

She crouched now, ready to pounce, and as Rook looked at the impossibly strong muscles, tensed and armed under shining, brown fur, he suddenly knew that the assumption that cougars don't attack men was itself a lie. No man in living memory or in tales passed down through the generations had ever faced a cougar alone, so how could they know? His spear would be lucky to even draw blood before she had his neck in her jaws. One man, no matter how brave or strong, is doomed against a mature cougar.

As they faced each other, waiting for Maker to flick his finger and put an end to his travesty, Rook realized that a low sound, a deep humming, was swelling behind him. The cougar heard it too. She stared, alarmed, but not at him. Her eyes had moved away from his, rising to look over his head. It sounded like a hundred bee swarms merged together into an angry black storm cloud. He desperately wanted to turn to look, but dare not take his eyes from the lady cougar.

The cougar suddenly opened her jaws and growled, a powerful, defiant challenge, and then the air sizzled, like boar fat dribbling onto the fire, and the ground in front of her suddenly flew upwards, as though a large, invisible rock had been hurled.

Confused and alarmed, the cougar took a few steps back, still growling a warning that now seemed as much pleading as belligerent. Another sizzle and blast of dirt and rocks, and she turned and ran away.

Amazed and apprehensive, Rook turned to see what had saved him, and he cried out and fell to his knees at what he found. It was impossible, but, unlike his mouth, his eyes didn't lie. A massive polished boulder, ten outstretched arms wide, hovered above him as though caught mid-bounce as it bounded down the slope, ready to squash him flat. Nothing held it up—Rook could clearly see the sky and horizon beneath it.

It was not possible, and therefore it must be Maker. Rook trembled and bowed his head, touching his forehead to the ground. All his life, Maker had manifested in subtle ways— curing his mother's fever after he'd watched his little sister eat the trout he'd caught, while he sat listening to his own growling, empty stomach, or punishing the family group by delaying the winter rains when they failed to banish his cousin Fargot for thrice forcing a fight with Galam, the last one ending in a blow to Galam's head that left him mute for two days. This flying boulder was anything but subtle. Maker had decided to make a personal appearance.

Rook whimpered as he whispered his apology. He hadn't realized just how serious lying to a cougar could be.

Staring into the dirt, he heard an answering whisper from above, but it was unintelligible, just a sigh. Was Maker pitying him, or was he expressing disappointment before dispensing punishment?

He flinched when he sensed movement on each side of him, but held still. Maker's will was unquestionable. He cried out, an involuntary outburst, when soft, firm hands grasped each arm. They pulled him upright, and other hands grabbed his ankles, lifting him so that he was suspended, facing the ground. Like Maker suspended above the ground as a boulder, he floated in the air, as the hawk rises in lazy circles above the hill.

For a moment, Rook thought that Maker was going to carry him away, far from his family group and tribe, banishing him to die alone and bereft, as was supposed to be Fargot's fate. Perhaps this was Maker's retribution for the family group's failure.

Rook's fate became clear before he had even finished that thought, however. Sudden, intense nausea overwhelmed him, and he gagged, and then vomited, spilling what little remained in his gut from the morning's meal of dandelion tubers and boar jerky. Maker wasn't going to carry him away for a protracted slow death from loneliness, but instead intended to torture and kill him, getting the punishment over with so that he could tend to other business.

The nausea torture gave way to intense dizziness, and then hallucinatory visions—images from his childhood, dreamlike scenes that had never occurred, and finally an indecipherable swirl of color, shape, and sound, an inexpressible flood of senses exploding from the world beyond the boundaries established when Maker had created the Earth.

Rook's last thought was gratitude to Maker for keeping his torture so short before his death.

∞

The heaven that greeted Rook when he woke was not what he expected, mostly since he hadn't thought that it was an option. Despite shaman Badgof's insistence otherwise, Maker was indeed a merciful god.

Rook had to admit, though, that he'd imagined heaven to be more … interesting than what now surrounded him. In fact, heaven was tiny. And he was the only member. Unease overtook him with the suspicion that this was possibly not heaven, that Maker was perhaps going to kill him with loneliness after all. The unease swelled to outright panic when he tried to lift his arms, and found them bound. His legs as well. In a fit of irrational terror, he began trashing, squirming frantically against the bindings that held him.

He froze when a voice said, "Be calm."

Whether a man or a woman, he couldn't tell, but they must have been right behind him. All he could see was pale walls, like untrodden snow. Maker might have brought him to a precisely chiseled ice cave, except that he wasn't cold at all.

"I will release you if you can stay calm," the voice said. "Can you stay calm?"

He nodded quickly, then realized that this person may not have seen that. "Yes," he said, glad that in heaven his voice still worked. "Where am I? Is this heaven?"

Rook felt something brush his wrists and ankles, and he found that he could raise his hands. They were the same ones he had before Maker killed him.

"You are in our boat," the voice said. "I am not confident what you mean by heaven, so I can't answer that."

Rook sat up and had another moment of unease when he saw that there was no entrance to this cave. Maker had apparently closed up the opening with more of this strange ice. Also, he was alone. Had they left? How could they? Perhaps the walls were so thin they could talk through them. "This is not a boat," he said loudly so they could hear him through the walls. A boat was a large, hollowed-out tree.

"Correct. This is not precisely a boat, but that is a word that comes closest. Try to imagine a very large boat that is covered against the rain."

He looked at the smooth, flat ice walls, and down at his bed, which was more warm ice—a slab of ice balanced on a pillar of the same. He tried, but he could not imagine how this cave was like a boat. "Are you ... Maker?"

"I have very limited experience with your language. Is it true that Maker is a god?"

"Uh, yes. Maker is *the* god. Other tribes have what they think are gods, but Maker is the only true—"

"No," the voice said. "We are not gods."

Rook blinked. Contrasted with that emphatic response, he realized how even the voice had been.

"What is your name?" the voice said, returning to a flat, soothing tone.

"You don't know?"

"We are not gods."

"My name is Rook."

"Very well, Rowek—"

"Not Rowek. That is my double-cousin from another family group. My name is Rook."

"Forgive me, Rook. As I said, your language is new to me. You are probably wondering why we—"

"If you're not Maker, then who are you?"

"That is not easy to explain in your language, Rook. We have come from far away. It has been a long time since we were last here, and there have been many changes with your people—"

"Do you mean the Natooma?"

"Can you tell me what the Natooma is?"

"It's not what the Natooma *is*, it's what the Natooma *are*."

"I don't understand, Rook."

"The Natooma are all of us—my close family, my cousins, my cousin's cousins. All of us."

"Rook, are you referring to your tribe? Your tribe is called Natooma?"

"Of course. My people, as you said."

"I see, Rook. I was referring to all of your people—the other tribes as well."

"They aren't people."

"Forgive me again, Rook. I believe that we are struggling with language. When we visit, we are interested in all the tribes."

"They aren't people," Rook insisted. He didn't want to seem difficult, but he also wanted this visitor to understand.

"Rook, perhaps this word, 'people,' is another word for Natooma, for your tribe?"

"No, but I think I understand your confusion. Natooma *is* the name of my tribe, but the other tribes are not like us. They're not people."

"How are they different, Rook?"

It was obvious. It had always been obvious. He never had to explain it before. "They're … not the same. They're stupid, and lazy."

"Rook, can members of your tribe breed with those of other tribes? Can men and women of different tribes have babies together?"

"Of course."

"Okay. I think I understand."

Rook wasn't sure this visitor did understand. He had a feeling this person didn't believe him. After all, on the rare occasions when they encountered other tribes, although never spoken, it was clear that members of the other tribes had the mistaken idea that *they* were better than the Natooma.

The voice said, "I'd like to explain why we have taken you."

Rook didn't answer. He was still trying to get a grip on where he was. If they were in a boat, then they would be on a river, but the nearest river was at least three days away. And in any case, that river was hardly large enough for a boat as big as this one must be.

The words of the voice sank in. "You've taken me? Where?"

"That's very difficult to explain in your language. I'm afraid that answer will have to wait until you have learned our language."

"You want me to learn your language?" That meant that they wanted him alive for some time. This was good news. He'd expected to be dead. "Okay," he said. He'd heard the languages of some distant tribes. This shouldn't be very difficult.

"Rook," the voice said, "don't you want to know why we took you?"

"I thought you were Maker, and you were punishing me for lying to the cougar."

"But we are not Maker."

"I know. I don't know why you took me."

"I have been trying to explain, Rook. We want you to help us. We will return someday, and then we'll need you to work with us as we meet your people—and when I say 'your people,' I mean all the tribes."

"Okay. I'm not sure how other tribes will greet me, but I'll do my best. Will we visit my family group?" Maybe they'd let him stay once he'd talked to the other tribes. He wondered if his family group would accept him as a man, or whether he'd have to go out again on transition.

"Rook, this is very difficult. It's not possible for you to understand yet what I'm about to tell you, but when we return, all of your family group—everyone you know—will have died."

"What! Why ... why would you do that?"

"Rook, do you think I am saying that we are going to kill them?"

"Yes. Or, who else?"

"No, Rook. Nobody is going to kill them. The reason they will have died is that much time will have passed. Not for you. For you, it will seem like just, as you would say, a handful of moon cycles."

"I ... I don't understand."

"I know, Rook. It is difficult. You will understand once we teach you our language."

"Will I sleep for all those new moons that my family will see and I won't? Like the bear in winter?"

"No, Rook. You will have to just trust me for now. I understand that this is difficult, and probably disheartening, but I wanted you to understand."

Why? he wondered. *Because ...?* "Can you take me back now if I don't want to go?

"I am sorry, Rook. That is not possible. Even if we chose to do that, many cycles of the sun would have passed before we returned. In any case, it is not possible."

"I have no choice, then."

"That is correct, Rook. I am sorry."

Rook stared at the featureless white walls, imaging sitting in this room for a handful of new moons. He was going to need this person, whoever it was, to talk with him. "Can I begin learning your language now?"

"Rook, that pleases me greatly. You should rest first, however. Lie down."

He didn't want to lie down. He'd just be thinking of his family that he will never see again. And the four white walls.

"Please lie down, Rook."

He sighed and lay back. His thoughts seemed to freeze, replaced with the formless swirls and colors, and then blackness.

∞

Rook woke and opened his eyes. For a moment, he thought that a warm rain was approaching, the way the sky always turns milky white beforehand. Then he remembered and sat up. The bare, white walls of the strange cave still surrounded him, but a bowl now sat on a pedestal that hadn't been there before.

"Hello, Rook," the familiar voice said.

He rubbed his eyes, feeling grainy, like he did the morning after hunting possums far into the night with his brother. He looked at his legs, and felt his chest. His deerskin jerkin and pants were gone, replaced with a thin, gray material, so fine, it could have been made from woven spider webs.

Someone had obviously opened the cave while he slept.

"Where are my clothes?" he asked.

"Your clothes were appropriate for your previous life. These are more suited for your new one."

My previous life, Rook thought. That was a kick in the gut. "You came into the cave."

"Yes. We also washed you."

He could see that. His hands were as clean as after he'd been swimming. Maker! They'd even cut back his fingernails. "While I was asleep?"

"Yes."

Now, that was a disturbing idea. "Why didn't I wake up?"

"Rook, we made you sleep very deeply."

"That was the jumble in my head."

"Probably, yes. Besides making you sleep, the brain-hand creates unintentional distributed activity."

He thought that he must have heard wrong. "Somebody stuck their hand in my brain?"

"No, Rook. Not a hand. Something invisible. It's the closest I can describe it in your language. You'll grasp it better when you learn ours."

"I still don't understand why you had to make me sleep."

"Rook, there is much that you can't understand yet. Again, many things will become clear once you've learned our language."

"That still doesn't explain why I had to sleep."

The voice usually didn't pause before answering. "I believe that we would make you uncomfortable, Rook."

"Why?"

"Rook, you have never seen anything like us. You would probably find us intimidating."

Some women of the Baktoomi tribe hunted with the men. Like men, they painted their faces with stalking masks, and carried spears. Rook had found this intimidating. He wondered if the person behind the voice was odd like that. He was confident he could get used to whatever strange clothes or body paint they wore. For now, though, they could stay behind the wall.

In fact, maybe they were intimidated by *him*!

"Rook," the voice of the hiding person said, "there is food in the bowl. I expect that you will find it quite bland, but it should be nourishing for your immediate needs. With time, we can experiment with different flavors and textures."

He slid off the ice-bed and examined the contents of the bowl. It looked like cooked buckwheat, formed into small bite-sized balls. He picked one up and smelled, but it might as well have been made from wood. He nibbled at it. He had never before tasted anything with no flavor at all. This wasn't food. He frowned, and put the rest of the ball back in the bowl.

"It is unappetizing Rook?" the voice said.

He nodded, staring at the bowl. He was very hungry and tempted. He picked up the ball and put the whole thing in his mouth. He chewed the tasteless mud and forced himself to swallow.

"Besides taste," the voice said, "there are an unknown number of ingredients that your body will need."

"Ingredients?" he said, popping another ball into his mouth. Although doing nothing to satisfy his hunger, the balls at least provided a mollifying sense of *something* in his stomach.

"Rook, your body is used to a wide variety of plants, each of which might contain food-things that you need. You took this for granted, but we'll have to duplicate them as we go along. There may be times when you don't feel well, and you must tell me so that we can try to find out what food-thing you are missing. This is important. Do you understand?"

"Yes," he said, looking at the next ball. Apparently, shaman Badgof had been right. When apprenticing as a boy, the spiritual chief had memorized a long list of plants—roots, seeds, stems and leaves—along with a complicated set of rules about priority and frequency. These rules had been given by Maker long ago. While the men went off hunting, shaman Badgof would accompany the women to make sure they gathered what the rules dictated. Many times, the hunters returned and groaned collectively when told that the women had been instructed to pass up delicious cherries or blueberries in order to find bitter burdock.

Rook sighed and methodically moved the balls from the bowl to his mouth, and down to his stomach.

∞

"Run fast," Rook offered.

"Not quite," the hiding voice said. "The word indeed means to move quickly, and it includes a sense of urgency, yet at the same time extreme caution."

He was getting a headache again. He had already learned at least two-to-the-eighth words, but most of those were objects, and Hiding Voice could show him pictures of those on the wall. Now Hiding Voice was including what he called "action" words, and each one denoted subtle complexities that at times seemed completely inexplicable to Rook.

"Shall I demonstrate?" Hiding Voice said.

Rook took a deep breath and nodded. He closed his eyes against the coming storm. Dancing colors and nonsense sounds contracted, seeming to rush together to form a flaming hot pebble at the base of his skull. He suddenly lost his balance and put his hands out to steady himself. That sometimes happened when Hiding Voice came in with the brain-hand. Emotions flailed: anger, sadness, jealousy—of what he didn't know—fear, joy, and then settled on something else, something different. This was the word Hiding Voice wanted him to learn. Rook suddenly felt an irresistible need to get away, to sprint off, but if he wasn't careful, if he didn't choose his steps and path prudently, he would come to great harm. "Okay," he said. "I've got it."

The fiery stone, along with the alien emotion, was instantly gone, leaving Rook, as always, struggling a moment to regain a sense of normalcy. His headache pounded a bit harder.

"Rook, what is two-to-the-second plus two-to-the-third?"

He pressed the heels of his palms into his eye sockets. Numbers. He knew that his headache was going to now grow to be "monumental"—a new word. He couldn't use the numbers he'd learned as a child. Hiding Voice had tried to explain that once he got the hang of their system, calculations would be much easier. That was yet another new word, "calculation."

Beneath the heels of his palms, behind his tired eyes, back in his brain, Rook imagined two-to-the-second, which was four. He mentally held up four fingers, and then eight fingers—two-to-the-third. "Twelve," he said, removing his hands and opening his eyes.

"Very good, Rook, but that is your old word, not your new one."

He stared at his toe. When they'd taken his clothes, they'd also taken his moccasins, leaving him barefoot. There was no need for foot protection now, Hiding Voice had told him.

"Rook?" the voice said.

He nodded, still staring. Twelve was between base 1, which is eight, and base 2, which is sixteen. So, the answer would be "Base one, point ..." twelve minus eight was, "four."

"Base-one-point-four, that is correct, Rook. But you counted on your fingers, didn't you, Rook?"

He looked up from the study of his toe. "Did you use the brain-hand?"

"No, Rook. The brain-hand can't discern that level of thought, and, besides, you would have known. Rook, you moved your fingers slightly as you calculated. Don't you see, Rook? Calculation wasn't even necessary for this problem."

Hiding Voice was right. They'd gone over this before. When adding any number that was a base to a smaller number, the answer was simply the base, followed by the first number as the fraction. That was a new word, "fraction," that had given him powerful—no, "monumental"—headaches.

He turned his gaze back to his big toe.

"Rook," the voice said, "are you discouraged?"

He nodded.

"Rook, I think you are mostly just tired. You should sleep, now." The timbre of Hiding Voice changed subtly when it continued, like his mother's had when, after the point of his spear would fall off because he hadn't wound the strap properly, and his older cousin would call him a girl-boy—the occasional male child in the wider tribe who preferred to play with girls, even dressing like them. "Rook," the voice said, "you should know that I admire your degree of stamina and persistence. You are an unusually good student."

He swung his gaze from his big toe to the wall, where he imagined the voice was hiding. He certainly didn't feel like a good student—he felt like an idiot. But it was good to hear.

"Time to sleep, Rook."

He lay back, and, as the hypnotic dance of colors and shape grasped his mind, he thought about what Hiding Voice had said: "You are an unusually good student." He wanted to ask, "There are others?" but the irresistible pull of the brain-hand dragged him down into deep slumber.

Chapter 2

Rook made a face, and spit the nibble back into the bowl with the rest of the green balls.

"Not satisfactory?" Hiding Voice said.

He had to think a moment. Hiding Voice now spoke only in his own language—Rook had decided that Hiding Voice was a "he"—and Rook had to search his memory for "satisfactory" until he found the meaning. "It tastes like ..." There was no word in Hiding Voice language, at least not that he'd learned. "It tastes like puke," he said reverting to his own.

Hiding Voice normally corrected him for speaking in his own tongue, but this time he let it go. "Rook, would you say that it is too bitter, or too sweet?"

"Neither," he replied in Hiding Voice language. "It's somewhere between the pink balls and the brown cubes, the ones I said tasted like excrement."

"I see. Thank you, Rook. Could you try to eat at least half? They contain a vitamin essential for your health."

He eyed them, his stomach gearing up to post a protest. "Can't you put the vitamins in the blue sticks? I could at least get them down."

"We will try, Rook. But in the meantime, could you try some more of these? Your lack of appetite could actually be caused by a deficiency of one of these vitamins."

He picked up another ball, closed his eyes, and pushed it into his mouth. *It doesn't taste like puke*, he told himself. But it did. He didn't really understand what a vitamin was, but since

Hiding Voice had said that it was a type of molecule that his body needed, he'd decided to put vitamins aside until he understood molecules.

And, of course, molecules were made up of atoms, which were made up of sub-atomic particles, which were themselves divided into individual or collections of quantum particles.

It was almost easier to comprehend the swirling colors of the brain-hand. He had decided to concentrate instead on something he could grasp—how blood flowed through his body, picking up oxygen along the way in his lungs. But since Hiding Voice had told him that oxygen was another type of molecule, Rook felt like he was following a circular path in the snow.

"Thank you, Rook" Hiding Voice said.

The bowl still contained more than half the balls, but if Hiding Voice was satisfied, he certainly was as well.

"I think some exercise would be good now, Rook," Hiding Voice said.

"Okay. I hope you enjoy it. It's good for you, you know," he said, mimicking his host.

"I think you know that I meant you, Rook."

One of the many things he missed was sharing humor. No matter how much he tried, he was never able to get Hiding Voice to join in.

He turned to the hated corner. They—whoever "they" were that entered the cave while he slept—had configured the corner with climbing steps and a pull-up bar for this wake cycle. The most despised enemy was a set of foot stirrups that forced him to run, at first, slowly, and then faster and faster until he could hardly catch his breath. Nearly as bad were two flexible vines that he grasped in each hand and pulled and swung in different directions as instructed by Hiding Voice. As each session progressed, Rook was sure that the vines began to pull back, eventually leaving him lying on the ground panting.

Some time ago—a new moon's worth, at least—he had rebelled and refused to grasp the ends of the vines. After coaxing him, Hiding Voice went away. At first, Rook had reveled in the luxury of simply lying on the ice bed and doing nothing—not learning about numbers and the workings of his body, nor sweating for no reason other than that it "was good for him," nor even forcing foul-tasting muck down his throat. It didn't take long, though, for Rook to get bored. He tried to sleep, but he wasn't tired or sleepy, and had just lain there, thinking about how featureless his cave was. He had finally sat up and called out to Hiding Voice, but there was no response. He lay back down, but the blank, white roof seemed to mock him about his utter dependence on Hiding Voice.

In the end, Rook had promised Hiding Voice that from then on, he would try his best to follow directions— "suggestions," as Hiding Voice called them.

Rook stared at the exercise steps. He knew that as soon as he stepped up, a new step would form out of the wall and slide down, so that he'd have to step up onto that one, and then another one, on and on, each step sliding down a bit faster than the previous, until the sweat poured down his face—the whole torturous point, according to Hiding Voice.

He walked over and stepped up. As the endless stream of steps rolled down, forcing him to step up, step up, step up, Hiding Voice said, "You find this monotonous, Rook?"

"What do you think?"

"I think you do."

"You think correctly."

"Tell me if this perhaps helps, Rook," Hiding Voice said. Suddenly, instantaneously, the wall before him opened up, and he was looking out into a dense forest, sunlight dappling the ground with joyful splotches of sunlight. Two red-patterned butterflies weaved a lazy, meandering dance together.

Rook fell back with a cry, and the forcefully rising step catapulted him, so that he tumbled backwards. He landed on a spongy, accommodating floor, a floor that had been solid a moment ago. As he lay there, stunned, he felt the soft floor lift and become firm again.

He rolled over and jumped to his feet. The forest was still there, whiling away a lazy afternoon in complete silence, as though Rook's ears were full of water. "What ...?" he started to say, completely at a loss to find words in Hiding Voice's language.

"I am sorry, Rook. I should have given you a warning. As you have no doubt guessed, this is not an actual forest."

He hadn't guessed. He had thought it was a real forest. He *still* thought it was.

"This is just an image, Rook, photons created in combinations and frequencies to appear like what you'd see if there were an actual forest before you."

"Photons," Rook said as he reached over the now-still steps. His hand came to rest against a hard, flat surface—the wall. Beyond his hand, the forest lay, as though on the other side of a sheet of clear ice.

"We talked about photons three sleep cycles ago, Rook."

"A quantum of electromagnetic energy," he repeated distractedly from rote memory, sliding his hand across the invisible wall, the forest beyond clearly an illusion. He had no idea what either a quantum, an electromagnetic, or an energy was. Hiding Voice had assured him that it would eventually all make sense.

"That's correct, Rook. Very good. Now, shall we continue with the exercise?"

Rook stepped up, and up, and up enthusiastically now. He had something to *look* at. He was elated, the sweat dribbling down his temples now a pleasant distraction. When the steps finally slowed and stopped, he lay on his back on the floor, and then sat up so that he could see the photon forest.

"That was a good workout, Rook," Hiding Voice said. "It's now time to talk about your long sleep."

Rook was still mesmerized by the forest. It was as though a dark thunder storm had passed in the night to reveal a fresh spring morning. "Long sleep?" he murmured.

"We talked about this at the beginning, Rook. It will be two-to-the-eighth days until we return to Earth. You don't want to be awake all that time."

He blinked. He looked at the forest. A doe stepped cautiously into the clearing, followed by her clumsy, wobbly young fawn. He'd just been handed a stupendous gift. The photon forest transformed his prison ice cave into a comfortable viewing platform, safe from prowling cougars. "Long sleep?" he repeated. He wanted to ask Hiding Voice why he had waited so long to give him this gift, but it didn't matter now.

He was going to sleep. For a long time.

∞

"Rook."

The tribal spring festival continued, but Rook was leaving—not on foot, not walking away through the scrub, but flying up and away, like a bird. The dancers, the clappers filling a circle around them, the fire tenders, rotating the buffalo shanks on spits—all of them became smaller and smaller, and Rook's heart ached at the parting.

"Rook," the voice said again.

He opened his eyes, and the dream dissolved. Where, by Maker, was he? The world was buried in a dense fog, but a fog that shown pure white. A memory of something like this was just beginning to form when the fog suddenly, instantly, lifted, revealing a thick forest. The speed at which the fog dissolved left Rook perplexed. Further, this was no forest he knew of. He recognized some of the trees, but many were foreign— similar to maples, but whose branches angled out instead of up.

"Rook," the voice said, "can you hear me?"

The voice, though, was completely familiar. Whose was it?

He was lying on his back, and he sat up. Or, he at least tried. His head filled with sparkles, like those that glittered on a sunny, wind-blown river, and he lay back, confused and a little frightened.

"Rook, it's time to wake up. But you must take it slowly. Rest awhile until you feel fully conscious."

He realized that he understood the voice, even though it wasn't using words.

No. That wasn't quite right. It was using words, just not real ones.

He remembered. It wasn't another dream. He was in a big boat, paddling far away from his home.

No, that wasn't right either. He'd been asleep for a long time. Before that, the voice had explained many things, among them, that the boat was more like a seed pod, containing air where there was no air, and that the Earth was actually a big ball, and that they were leaving it behind, like walking many new moons away from a tiny grain of sand.

He had a headache. He wasn't sure if it had been there when he woke, or if it was simply all the information crammed in and pressing to get out.

He sat up, this time slowly. He felt terrible, weak and achy, like he had as a child when the fever had passed through the family group. "I'm sick," he said.

"Rook," Hiding Voice said, "please use proper language. Your sickness will pass. Your body has been dormant for a long time, and needs to recover. When you can stand, drink the liquid."

He saw the familiar white bowl sitting on the white food pedestal, incongruous against the forest, which he now knew wasn't real. "Okay," he said in Hiding Voice's language. Remembering all the new words seemed to aggravate his headache, making it swell, like the fur of a threatened bobcat.

He slid off the sleeping platform, and clutched the edge for a moment, thinking he was going to collapse. The sparkles evaporated, and he took a tentative step forward. The bowl suddenly beckoned to him. He realized that he was immensely thirsty. Three more staggering steps, and he lifted the bowl to his lips. The liquid was like the breath of Maker, even though Hiding Voice had insisted that Maker was just a story that served a useful purpose for the tribe.

Rook was amazed at the effect of drinking. Most of the feelings of sickness had been simple thirst. Indeed, he felt strength returning, and he put the bowl down and swung his arms back, stretching.

"Rook," Hiding Voice said, "once you have finished the soup, rest a little, and we will begin your next lessons."

Images of little dots dancing together, called atoms and molecules, and much larger dancing balls called stars and planets pushed forward through the diminishing headache. What he really wanted to do was to sit on the ground and stare at the forest. "Are we going to talk about how jiggling atoms make other atoms jiggle?" he asked. "Heat flow," he quickly added before Hiding Voice could correct him. This was supposed to explain why a rock sitting in the sun felt warm, but he hadn't gotten the connection yet.

"That will have to wait, Rook."

"What, then?"

"You must learn to pronounce new words."

"More vocabulary?"

"Not my language, Rook. This is a language completely new to you."

"Why? Why should I learn this?"

"Rook, this is a language of people of your own Earth."

"My own Earth …?"

"Rook, we have returned."

∞

"*Pétros*," Rook repeated.

"That's better," Hiding Voice said. "Try it again."

He repeated the word after hearing it once more. "What does it mean?" he asked.

"As I've already explained, Rook, you don't need to know that."

"I know. I'm just curious."

"There's much to learn, Rook. Meanings will simply make it harder."

It seemed silly to learn a language without meanings. Hiding Voice had insisted that this didn't matter. Rook didn't even know how many words he'd already learned to say—two-to-the-seventh at least, probably more. He simply repeated them after Hiding Voice, one after another, on and on. He was getting the gist of the pronunciation nuances, to the point where he could practically repeat any new word Hiding Voice uttered.

"That's enough," Hiding Voice said at last. "Eat and rest. Then you will be returning to Earth."

He blinked. This was typical Hiding Voice. No warning, no intimation, just the pronouncement that, before he even had time to think about it, he would be going home.

This was it, the promised homecoming. It wasn't really home of course, since, as unbelievable as it seemed, many, many season cycles had passed since he'd left.

But at least it would be a real forest, with smells and sounds, and a breeze.

Oh, how he missed a wet breeze.

∞

"Wake up, Rook."

He opened his eyes. The unreal forest was gone, the world was again a barren white. Instinctively, he tried to sit up, and grunted when his attempt resulted in nothing other than alarm at being pinned down. This had been explained by Hiding Voice beforehand, but he'd forgotten in the moment. Even his wrists were secured. Despite the forewarning, he felt prickly barbs of panic.

"Are you ready, Rook?"

He sighed. "I just woke up." Peering around, he could see subtle differences in the texture of his white surroundings, enough to gauge the surfaces. Compared to his room, this space was tiny, hardly larger than a hibernating bear cave. Hiding Voice had called this a shuttle, a smaller boat that would be taking him down from far above the ground where there was no air.

"Is this a problem, Rook?"

"No. It's just …"

"What is the problem, Rook?"

"I get no time."

"I don't understand, Rook."

"It's like … every time you wake me, there's something immediately waiting that I have to do."

"I think I understand, Rook. You need some idle periods? Maybe some time to do mental preparation?"

"I guess … yes! That's exactly it."

"Okay, Rook. We'll keep that in mind. Now, are you ready?"

How could he know? All that Hiding Voice had told him was that the shuttle trip would last two-to-the-eighth heartbeats, and that somebody would be waiting at the other end to tell him what to do. Considering that he was immobile, securely strapped in place, he couldn't imagine what readiness there was to be achieved. "Yeah," he said sarcastically, even though Hiding Voice never seemed to react to tones, whether frustrated, angry, or sarcastic.

There was one thing he was ready for—he was intrigued to meet whomever was waiting down there. It would be his first glimpse of his kidnappers. Or generous hosts, depending on his mood.

He hadn't finished this thought when he was pressed down. An invisible hand pressed harder. And harder. The restraints were superfluous. He wouldn't have been able to lift his arms in any case.

Then, suddenly, he was floating, like when he was a small boy and his father lifted him off the ground, and tossed him, laughing, into the air.

Then the pressing hand returned, but this time from below. All the restraints felt as though they were inexorably tightening. He understood that the pressing hand was a metaphor, that the force trying to rip away the restraints was an illusion, a result of the shuttle craft's movements.

But the sense that a hand was pushing him was inescapable. A big hand. A big calloused hand.

Then he was floating.

Then the hand again pushed against his chest, at first with vigor, but slowly letting up, until it was gone. He lay there with normal weight. An instant later, the restraints were gone, and Rook rubbed his wrists where they had grasped him.

"You are on the ground, Rook," Hiding Voice said, "back on Earth."

He took a deep breath and nodded. This was it. Home.

"It is night, however," Hiding Voice continued. "We must wait for dawn."

"What?" Rook exclaimed, making no effort to hide his dismay. He wanted to remark on the irresponsible lack of planning, and would have, except that the familiar swirling colors of the brain-hand pulled him down into sleep.

∞

"Time to wake," Hiding Voice said.

Rook opened his eyes. This must have been a short sleep. There was no confusion—he knew that he lay in the shuttle, waiting for dawn.

"Okay, Rook, ready to leave?"

He snorted. "What happened to idle periods and mental preparation?"

"I'm sorry, Rook, but there is not time for that."

"You could have woken me earlier."

"That is true, Rook, but that opportunity is past. Please prepare to leave."

As before, he couldn't imagine what preparation there was to make, and he knew that when Hiding Voice said "please," it meant that he had no choice.

He was rotating. The bed he was lying on was tilting up, and his feet were soon taking his weight. Maybe that was what he had to be ready for.

He stood there, staring at the white surface, wondering what to do. He reached out and placed his palm against the wall. It was smooth, and surprisingly warm. The sensation lasted only an instant, and then his hand pushed out against air.

The wall had disappeared, but not completely, just an oblong hole a little taller and wider than him. He was looking off towards a horizon, visible as a thin golden glow sandwiched between blackness below and a pale dark blue sky above, fading to black overhead, where sharp points of the brightest stars still shone. The view, gazing into a distance he hadn't known in so many new moons, caught his breath, but only for a moment, for that breath brought home the Earth—his Earth—more vividly than a promising dawn horizon, with fleeting hints of sage, chamomile, and—Maker be—dirt. How he missed dirt. Tendrils of a morning breeze teased his bangs, and his vision blurred with tears.

From somewhere off to his left, a buzzing, like a bumblebee, came near. A vague thought that perhaps he should lean back, away from the insect, nudged him, but he was too mesmerized by long-lost sensations to heed.

"Step out of the shuttle, Rook," a tiny voice said beside him.

It sounded like Hiding Voice, if he were talking through a hollow reed.

"We have limited time, Rook," the little voice said. "Please step out."

He obeyed the "please" and stepped forward, stumbling when his feet found that the ground lay a hand's width below the lip of the hole in the shuttle.

The buzzing took up a position between him and the shuttle opening. "Step away, Rook," the miniature Hiding Voice said.

The ground under his feet felt like sand, as though he was standing on a beach along the river, except that this sand was hard-packed. He'd gone bare-foot the whole time in his white room, but he'd woken in the shuttle wearing an odd moccasin that had no draw-strings, but rather enclosed his feet snugly, extending up his ankle, and under his pants. He stepped forward cautiously in the darkness, but his feet found no obstacles, just the crunch of long-dry sand. He sensed something move behind him, a slight tremor in the ground, and a sudden waft of air. He turned, but could see nothing in the pre-dawn darkness. Where the bulk of the shuttle had been, however, he now saw a few stars along the opposite horizon. Above him, far off, and gaining distance, he heard the rising whistle of an arrow cutting the air. The shuttle was speeding off to the big boat—the starship—somewhere up there where there was no air.

"Come, Rook," the tiny voice said. "We have some distance to go before the sun comes up."

The buzzing started away, and Rook followed. The golden line along the eastern horizon had swelled, and he was beginning to make out his surroundings. They seemed to be on a flat plain. Scattered bushes marched off as far as the dim light could reveal.

So much for returning to a real forest. There wasn't a tree in sight. And, he'd have to wait for that wet breeze. He could tell by the sharp outlines on the horizon and the crystal-clear points of starlight that the air was very dry.

"Um, hello?" Rook said.

He heard the buzzing return. "Yes, Rook?"

"I, uh …"

"What is it, Rook?"

"Are you the same person?"

"The same as whom?"

He'd never referred to Hiding Voice by any name. There'd been no need. The voice was there whenever he spoke. "The person on the big boat—the starship. The person that always talks to me."

"No, Rook. Your question implies something not quite true, but no, I am not the same entity as that which you have been speaking with on the starship."

"Then, who are you?"

"That could take a long time to answer adequately—time we don't have now, but I will tell you that I am what you might think of as a monitor. You could think of yourself as an ambassador for your short visit."

These were new words for Rook. "I don't understand."

"I was left here on the starship's last visit. To observe your planet."

"Really?"

"Yes, Rook. Do you find that surprising?"

He didn't think that Hiding Voice would have caught the surprise in his voice. "I mean, you've been here all this time. Hasn't it been, like, two-to-the-twelfth season cycles?"

"Yes. Nearly four thousand years."

"Thousand?"

"A thousand is ten-to-the-third. Your people use a base-ten system of counting, because that's how many fingers you have."

Rook was doing the math. Ten was between two-to-the-third, and two-to-the-fourth. This would take some getting used to. "You've been alive that long?" he said.

"Again, Rook, your question implies something not true, but, yes, I have been operating since then. I am sorry, but we must keep going if we are to succeed."

They started forward. It was now light enough to see the sparse ground clearly, and they picked up the pace.

"Where are we going?" Rook asked.

"To meet a great general."

Rook had learned that word. "An army leader?"

"Yes."

"Why?"

"To give him a gift."

"You need me for this?"

"Yes, Rook."

"Why?"

"Rook, your people don't know about me. They wouldn't understand."

And I do? Rook thought. "Why are we giving him a gift?"

"It is a good thing."

"Okay. That doesn't really answer the question, though, does it?"

"Perhaps not, Rook. This gift is a powerful weapon that this great general can use for the good of your people."

Rook wasn't sure what he expected this new guide to look like. Judging by the tiny voice, he would have guessed possibly a thin little man, maybe a Binkle, a mythical beast the size of a raccoon that populated stories told to children of his tribe. As the dawn light strengthened, however, he found that there was nothing in front of him. The little voice seemed to come out of thin air. But then a sliver of sun peeked over a low ridge, and suddenly a dazzling little ball, like an oversized golden dandelion fuzz, was hovering in the air five paces ahead of him.

Was this …? Could it be …?

"Wait!" he called.

The indistinct golden ball stopped, then floated a few paces towards him. "Yes, Rook?" the ball said.

It was! In the growing sunlight, Rook saw that it looked like a ball only because the translucent wings were blurred with speed.

His guide, the being to whom his life was now entrusted, was a hummingbird.

Blaine C. Readler

Chapter 3

"Dig here," the tiny voice of the hummingbird said, hovering over a patch of sandy dirt no different than any other across the endless plain.

The sun was fully up now, and Rook was sweating inside the white outfit that fit him so closely, it was like the skin of a snake, except that, unlike that of a snake, his wasn't about to molt any time soon. Off in the distance, undulating in the rising heat, the city could be seen, rectangular structures, brown and gray, the color of the ubiquitous dirt from which they were made. Tiny Voice had said that this was their destination, and Rook imagined that he would collapse before reaching it.

First, though, he had to dig, to retrieve the general's gift.

"What are you doing, Rook?" tiny voice said.

"Looking for something to dig with, maybe a stone or a stick—"

"That's not necessary. You can use your hands."

Rook shrugged and plopped down on his knees as Tiny Voice moved aside. Almost immediately, his fingers felt something soft, and he pulled out a bundle wrapped in course cloth.

"There are two items," Tiny Voice said. "One is small, so be careful."

He laid the bundle down, unwrapped the cloth, and gasped. He'd never seen anything so strange. And beautiful. The starship was odd—his all-white cave room, and unreal forests—but this was fantastic. "What *is* it?" he whispered.

"It's a cup."

He could see that. The general shape was the same as the one often waiting when he woke, but this ... he would never use it for something so crude as drinking. It was worthy of Maker (even though there was no Maker). "What is it made from?" he asked, touching it with his fingertip, and then withdrawing quickly when he saw its reflection on the polished surface, afraid he'd broken some taboo.

"Gold."

"Gold?"

"It's a soft metal, revered by your people."

He could see why. *He* revered it. "What are these?" he asked, pointing to squiggly marks along the bottom.

"Persian lettering—they represent words in that language."

Rook glanced at Tiny Voice. "Is this the language I've been practicing?"

"No. You have been practicing the language of the general, but he admires this culture that he has conquered. Rook, we must hurry. Find the other item."

He broke his gaze from the magical cup. He found another small bundle, almost lost among the cloth wrapping. Whereas the larger bundle wrapping was woven from thick thread, this material was more like his own clothes—a texture so fine, he had to look closely to see any definition. Inside, he found what looked like a stubby honey locust thorn, as long as a joint of his finger. He glanced at Tiny Voice.

"Put it in your ear," the little alien bird said.

"In my *ear*?"

"Yes. It won't hurt you. It's waiting."

It's waiting? he thought. Perhaps this was a phrase without literal meaning. He held it up and peered at the featureless little spike looking for some hint of its function.

"Put it in your ear, Rook."

He was taught as a child, with slaps for emphasis, not to stick objects in his ear. It was like asking him to dribble sand into his open eye.

"Please place it in your ear, Rook."

Finally the "please." Time was up. "Which end first?"

"It doesn't matter."

He slowly inserted it halfway.

"It can go farther," Tiny Voice said.

Rook snorted and pushed it in a bit more, then yelped when he felt it move. He tried to yank it back out, but it swelled to fill the canal, and the protruding end flattened and seemed to resist his prodding.

"Leave it be, Rook. We must be going."

He stood staring. Tiny Voice was talking inside his head.

"It's a communication device," Tiny Voice explained.

He waved his hand alongside his head, making sure there wasn't another alien bird that had snuck up. "It repeats what you say?" he wondered.

"In a way, yes. We must go now."

Tiny Voice flew away, and Rook followed. "What's the name of this place?" Rook asked.

"Babylon. At one time, this used to be the capital of the greatest empire on Earth, but that was two hundred years ago. This great general has decided to use the city for his new, even greater, empire."

"What is an empire?"

"Multiple nations under one ruler."

"A nation is like a tribe?"

"Yes. But since your time here, the tribes have settled down and created complex civilizations suited for hierarchical societies based on agriculture."

Rook walked on.

"You don't understand much of that, do you, Rook?"

He shook his head.

"Let me explain."

Rook tried his best to grasp the concepts, and, in the end, he decided that people of Earth had become ants. Tiny Voice finished by saying, "Rook, once we arrive, try not to act surprised at what happens."

"What's going to happen?"

"I can't predict. But you can be confident that I won't let you get hurt."

Rook didn't see how a little bird could protect him, but his head was overflowing with hierarchies, and the strange concept of keeping whole families of animals always at your camp, to kill and eat whenever you liked, that he didn't pursue it. Instead, he asked about something that had bothered him since digging up the bundle. "You said that this cup, is a weapon. How can that be?"

Like Hiding Voice, the little bird always responded with no hesitation, and so even the slightest pause, like now, stood out. "There are many types of weapons, Rook. Spears and arrows are obvious ones. However, anything that can influence the long-term course of events can be used as a weapon."

He could see that. "This cup can do this?"

"If the general uses it properly, yes."

"Is it magical?"

"Rook, you know there is no magic. Some weapons are subtle, their power residing in their hidden meaning."

He sighed. He guessed what came next. "It's a symbol?"

"In a way, yes."

He'd come to a dead end. He should have known it would end in symbolism. Hiding Voice had tried to explain symbolism. He had compared it to the designs that Rook's tribe painted on their faces when hunting, but try as he would, Rook couldn't connect the obvious and simple joy of seeing a tribal signature with the squiggly characters that Hiding Voice insisted represented words.

Rook decided to try a question with, presumably, a direct answer. "What is the name of this great general?"

"Alexander."

∞

"Remember," Tiny Voice said in Rook's ear, "don't look at me, and repeat exactly what I say."

Rook stood in the blistering sun as two men approached. He and Tiny Voice had arrived at the city sooner than he'd guessed. He had mistakenly associated the size of the buildings in the distance with ridges and mountains he was used to. Rook was prepared for changes after four thousand years, but these two approaching men were outlandish. They wore skirts, like women, and from their heads rose exaggerated crests, like a blue jay. As they got closer, he saw that, in fact, their heads were completely covered in metal, even along their cheeks, and the crest on top was artificial. He thought that this very odd and complicated decoration perhaps served the same purpose as his tribe's facial paint. If so, it must be difficult, and therefore valuable, to belong to this tribe.

The two men stopped twenty paces away, clearly concerned. One of them pulled a thick metal stick out from his belt, what Rook took to be a weapon. The man yelled something. Rook started to turn, but remembered that he wasn't supposed to look at Tiny Voice hovering out of view behind him. "Repeat this," his little bird companion said inside his ear.

Rook called out words he could pronounce without meaning.

The man with the metal stick glanced at his companion and shouted again.

"What does he want?" Rook said quietly.

"He wants you to lie on the ground," Tiny Voice said. "Repeat this."

He did, and in response, the man nodded to his companion, who drew his stick as well, and they stepped apart, clearly preparing to attack.

Even with the limited experience Rook had with metal, he suspected that those sticks could be fearsome weapons. "Should I lie down?" he said.

"No! That is the opposite message to convey. Repeat this."

His words only angered the two men. They stepped forward, holding the metal weapons in both hands. Tiny Voice had told him to be confident that he wouldn't get hurt. Rook was realizing that confidence wasn't something you could decide to have.

The men came closer and closer, moving apart, so that they were coming at him from opposite sides.

"Um," Rook said nervously, "maybe I should run?"

"Hold out your arm and point at one of the men," Tiny Voice said.

Maker! Rook thought, *Tiny Voice doesn't even see them!* He did as instructed, however, trying hard to keep his finger from shaking.

Along with the buzzing sound behind him, Rook heard a humming that swiftly rose in pitch, and an instant later, a flash of light splashed across the man's chest, just where Rook was pointing. The man's arms flew outward, the metal stick falling away, and he collapsed. He lay on the ground, writhing, and a small cloud of dust rose to envelope him.

Tiny Voice spoke, and Rook shouted the meaningless words. The second man stood, frozen in shock. "Now point at him," Tiny Voice said. The man dropped his sword and stepped back as Rook's arm swung towards him. Rook shouted another conveyed message, and the man nodded, and went to his companion, who now lay holding his head in his hands.

"What did we say?" Rook whispered.

"You told them who you are."

"That I came from a starship?"

"They wouldn't understand that. You said that you come from a place above the clouds, where regular people would immediately perish. They believe that you are a god."

"Like Maker?"

"Similar. Their gods mimic their family and social structure, and thus resemble normal people, like you."

"But, I'm not a god."

"No need to tell them that. It would only confuse them."

Rook was in no hurry to correct their mistaken belief. These men probably avoided using metal weapons against their gods.

∞

"What's happening?" Tiny Voice said in Rook's ear.

As they had approached the limits of the city, led by their two escort soldiers, the little bird had surreptitiously landed on Rook's arm and folded its wings flush with its body—as long as his thumb, and smooth as river-polished pebbles—and he had slipped the enigmatic beast into a breast pocket apparently made for the purpose.

"The two soldiers are arguing with other soldiers," he replied quietly. "People are starting to gather around. They seem curious, but also fearful."

Rook wasn't sure who was more fearful, him, or them. He hadn't imagined the city to be so huge. The square, hulking structures that loomed above him on all sides were as tall as trees. Tiny Voice had explained that these people had *built* these. To Rook, this city was far, far more impressive than his starship, which, after all, consisted of white walls and imaginary forests. The fact that the starship was able to travel great distances was probably something impressive, but like the tales of great ancestral bear hunts, it was just a story—not an experience—and the awe faded with time.

"They are arguing about which city gate to enter," Tiny Voice said, evidently able to hear through the cloth of the pocket. "Call out this word loudly," Tiny Voice instructed.

Rook's shout was more a nervous croak, but the effect was immediate. Their two escorts started off, calling impatiently to their companions who seemed skeptical, but fell in behind.

They soon came to a giant canyon, which Tiny Voice explained was the walls of a fortress on each side. Far above, walkways connected the two man-made cliffs. From these high vantage points, soldiers looked down, watching them pass. Rook stopped short when he turned his gaze forward again.

"Why are we stopping?" Tiny Voice said.

Rook stood speechless. Before them rose something so stupendous, he thought he was perhaps dreaming. Blocking their way was a huge blue cliff face, at least two trees tall. A massive arched doorway, wide enough for five people to pass side-by-side, was guarded on each side by soldiers. The blue cliff face, made from thousands of blue bricks, was breathtaking enough, but a myriad of strange, otherworldly animals clung to the sides. At first, he thought that they were pictures, but they had depth, protruding out from the vertical surface, as though they'd been killed and mounted somehow.

"Rook," Tiny Voice said, "why are we stopping?"

In fact, the escort soldiers had not, and now turned to watch him.

"Uh, it's ... hard to explain—a giant blue wall. It's, it's—"

"It is the Ishtar Gate, a tribute to the Babylonian goddess of both love and war. What are the soldiers doing?"

"They're, uh, just watching me."

"Rook, I told you not to seem surprised at anything. Hold your palms up, towards the wall, and shout this loudly."

Rook repeated and called out a series of nonsensical syllables, which bounced around the cavern walls, amplifying his invocation and rendering it far more commanding than he felt.

"Now, turn to the soldiers," Tiny Voice instructed, "and hold out your arms, as though expressing vindication."

The soldiers nodded slowly, glancing at the wall, and back to him. A rumbling moan rose from the citizens that now surrounded them, however, causing the soldiers to shout and threaten them with their swords, forcing them away from the archway, and motioning for Rook to proceed through.

As he walked beneath the high arch and into the inner city, Rook asked what he'd just called out. "You challenged Ishtar to confront you if she existed, and concluded that she indeed does not. The soldiers believe in their own gods, including you, but the citizens of the city are Babylonian, and do still worship Ishtar and their other gods. It is a hallmark of Alexander that he does not interfere with the cultures and religions of the nations he conquers. It is one reason he is such a successful empire builder."

"This cup will help with that?" Rook said distractedly as his wondering gaze danced from one architectural marvel to the next on both sides of the long, wide avenue that stretched before them.

Again that slight pause. "No, Rook. That is not the cup's purpose."

The citizens of Babylon continually gathered and massed on each side ahead of them, but melted back into the side streets as they came close, as though afraid of his blatant blasphemy.

Eventually, blocking the avenue—comprising its end, in fact—stood a building larger than the rest, but functional and almost bland. Some of the soldiers had run on ahead. The small remaining entourage, consisting of Rook and a half dozen soldiers in front and behind him, stopped before closed doors, two-men high. The soldiers stood, staring at the doors. Rook looked at them. He thought that they were maybe in a trance, like shaman Badgof during Maker-moon ceremonies, new moons when the sun's seasonal travels were lowest and highest in the sky. "What's happening?" Rook whispered.

"Alexander is probably getting ready. His soldiers believe that you are a god, but I doubt that the general will just take their word for it."

Rook started at the sound of loud creaking, and the doors swung ponderously inward, revealing darkness within. The escort soldiers remained motionless, staring into the black interior. With a barked order from somewhere within, they all started forward together, the ones in back nearly running Rook over before he fell into step.

As his eyes adjusted to the darkness, Rook saw that their path was dimly lit by torches mounted above eye level. They made several turns, with the torches guiding the way. Somebody had apparently placed them for just this purpose. They arrived at a large room, where two soldiers stood in the doorway, blocking their path. One of them called something loudly, and they stepped aside, revealing a man sitting in a large chair looking at them, a soldier flanking him on each side. The chair rested on a platform, so that the man, presumably Alexander, gazed slightly down at them. He wore a close-fitting shirt made of metal, and wide leather bands encircled both wrists, but otherwise, seemed unremarkable. In fact, lacking the engraved helmet and plumage crest, he appeared actually ordinary next to the soldiers he commanded.

Plain attire could not diminish the power manifest in his alert, ever-watchful eyes, however. This was a man who did not question his absolute authority. He gestured for Rook to come forward, and studied him intently, his eyes absorbing Rook's peculiar white clothes. Following Tiny Voice's instruction, Rook stopped at the edge of the platform. "Is this Alexander?" Rook whispered.

"Yes," Tiny Voice replied. "Please appear self-assured."

Rook glanced down at his breast pocket, caught himself, and looked back up at Alexander. "How, exactly, would you suggest I do that?"

"You can begin by not whispering."

Just then, Alexander said something, and Rook repeated Tiny Voice's unknowable words. "What did I say?" Rook whispered, ignoring Tiny Voice's suggestion.

"He greeted you, and you returned the salutation. Say this."

As he finished his recitation, Alexander's brow furrowed.

"You told him that you are pleased with his successes in conquering the world," Tiny Voice said. "This implies that you are at least an equal, and he is not used to such assumed perspective."

Alexander was already saying something. "He asks from where do you come," Tiny Voice explained, "and what people you command. You will respond by indicating that you command no one but yourself, and you come from the sky."

At this, one of Alexander's eyebrows went up. "He asks if you come as a god," Tiny Voice said. "By asking in this way, he neither confirms that he believes you are a god, nor does he necessarily deny your own belief. Your reply will simply state that your many powers derive not from this Earth."

Alexander's frown returned.

"He tells you," Tiny Voice said, "that you surely don't expect him to take your word at this. Rook, he obviously wants proof. Say this."

Alexander's eyes went wide, and he glanced quickly at his guard soldiers, whose expressions never wavered.

"What did I say?" Rook whispered.

"You told him that he has been constipated lately. Nobody knew this, of course. You told him that his drunken bouts are aggravating the problem. You must quickly follow with the gift presentation."

Rook mouthed Tiny Voice's words, and stepped up onto the platform, unwrapping the bundle as he went. The guard soldiers jumped forward, but retreated when Alexander motioned them back. Rook held out the cup, and repeated the long sequence, which Tiny Voice translated as he spoke.

"We the powerful who dwell above the clouds present this cup as a gift in recognition of your victories so far. Drinking from it has the power to change the course of human destiny. No enemy can stand against its clever use, but beware—a sword has two edges, and can cut both ways. A sip would spell doom for any normal mortal, so keep it safe from the foolish and unwary."

Alexander stared at the cup in Rook's hand, and his cautious gaze lifted to meet his. The general of an expanding empire reached out and took the cup, turning it over, admiring the fine details. He looked at Rook again and spoke.

"He asks how a cup can be so powerful," Tiny Voice said. "You will tell him that it is because it comes from you."

Alexander didn't seem convinced. "He asks how he is to use it," Tiny Voice said. "You will say that you wouldn't have given it to him if you didn't have confidence in his ability to wield it."

Alexander smiled wryly. He knew straight answers were not to be. He seemed to decide. He laid the cup in his lap, and raised both hands, proclaiming loudly.

"He calls for a feast in your honor," Tiny Voice said. "You will explain that you are grateful for his respect, but that your task is now complete, and you must return to the sky."

At this, Alexander actually seemed relieved. After all, entertaining a god who may or may not *be* a god could have been somewhat awkward.

His soldier escort fell into place again as Rook retraced his steps. At the doors, he paused and looked back. Alexander sat staring at the cup he held in both hands. Rook imagined that this is what it must be like when Maker contemplates the world he nurtures and rules.

If there were a Maker.

Outside, back on the long avenue, Tiny Voice instructed Rook to remove him from the pocket hiding place. After holding the smooth oblong body in his open palm long enough to intone some nonsense incantation, Rook tossed his guide high into the air. The escort soldiers gazed up as the little ebony object soared up and up, and never came down. Without another word, Rook started off again down the avenue, and now it was the soldiers who had to hustle to keep up. Tiny Voice was up there somewhere, too high to be seen, reconnoitering the way out.

Once through the Ishtar Gate, and on past the bewildering complexity of the outer city, arriving finally where the endless plain of scattered bushes patiently waited at the threshold of the last of the earth-colored cube buildings, the voice in his ear told Rook to stop. In words he didn't understand, he told the soldiers to go back, that he would proceed alone. They hesitated, glancing at each other until Tiny Voice told Rook to say two commanding words, at which point, the soldiers trotted away, back into their conquered city. "What did I say?" Rook whispered.

"You told them to leave or die. It was a baseless threat, but did them no harm."

He walked out into the arid expanse, and had hardly made a hundred paces when Tiny Voice said, "You have visitors, Rook."

He turned and looked back towards his exit from the city where a few soldiers and some dozens of citizens still lingered. "Not there," Tiny Voice said. "To your left."

"What is it?" Rook said. He wasn't sure he understood what he saw. There were a handful of men. And there were a handful of large animals, like deer, but heavier, with long flowing hair all down their necks, and long tails of the same texture. Weirdly, the men and animals were all jumbled together, as if the men were continually jumping up as high as the animals' backs. The puzzle resolved, and he saw that the men were riding on the backs of the animals.

"They are Persians," Tiny Voice said, "the conquered nation of the cup's design. The lead horse carries a Persian prince, invited along by Alexander as a liaison."

Rook didn't know what a liaison was, but he could guess that it represented some sort of cultural bridge. He also now knew the word for the animals the men were riding.

He waited as the squad of horse riders approached. In the lead, Rook saw, was indeed a man distinctive from the rest. Whereas the leader's companions wore plain knee-lengths shirts secured with wide leather belts, this man's clothes burst with blue and gold color. His calves and feet were bound with a golden weaved material, and atop his head he wore a helmet, more decorative than protective, since the metal didn't even cover his ears.

Rook stepped back as the Persian prince pulled his horse to a stop directly in front of him and drew a thin sword curved like the crescent of a new moon.

"Hold your ground," Tiny Voice said. "Please do not show fear."

He gazed up at the prince as dust kicked up by the horse settled on his shoulders. Rook could suppress outward signs of fright, but not the panic that swirled beneath his skin as this prince shouted angrily and raised the wicked thin sword to strike.

"Say this," Tiny Voice instructed.

Rook hesitated. The words that Tiny Voice gave him were completely unfamiliar, nothing like those he'd learned to speak with Alexander. He guessed that this must be the language of the prince. He did his best, and the prince seemed to understand, for he relaxed the sword, letting it fall to his side.

"You told him that you are not a god," Tiny Voice said. "He knows that you challenged and devalued Ishtar, and feels that he must confront you and prove to his own men his claim to divine succession."

The prince studied Rook. He looked at his men, and back down at him. He shook the reigns of his horse, and it walked forward.

"Stay where you are," Tiny Voice said.

Fighting every instinct of his being, Rook stood straight until the very nose of the horse was in his face, the warm animal breath washing down his chest. The prince lifted the sword and leaned forward, pressing the tip against Rook's chest. The sharp point hurt. The pressure increased as the prince pushed harder, and Rook was sure he was going to be impaled. Terror overcame him, and he jumped back.

"Please hold your ground," Tiny Voice said.

"He wants to kill me!" Rook whispered.

Tiny Voice didn't respond.

The prince urged his horse forward, and again the sword's tip came at him. Rook stepped back, but the horse kept coming. He stumbled on a rock and fell, and the sword's tip was above him. He rolled to the side and jumped up. The prince's eyes bore through him with satisfied determination as he shook the reigns and kicked the sides of his horse. Rook turned and ran. "He's going to kill me!" Rook yelled.

Silence haunted his inner ear.

He heard the thumping hooves, obviously catching him. "Help me!" Rook cried. He glanced back and saw that the horse was right behind, and then he tumbled, tripping on a bush. He felt thuds as hooves pounded the dirt all around him, miraculously missing him, and passed on. Before he was up on hands and knees, the prince turned the horse around, and came back. Rook knew it was useless. He could never outrun this animal.

But then the horse slid to a sudden stop, shaking its head. There, hovering right before it, was a shimmering ball, so bright, it was hard to look at. The horse backed up, despite the prince's efforts to stop it.

The blinding white light subsided, revealing Tiny Voice suspended inside the blur of translucent wings. "Say this," Tiny Voice said, "loudly."

Again, the words were unfamiliar, but, judging by the anger in his face, the prince obviously understood. He lifted his head in defiance.

"Again," Tiny Voice said.

This had little effect, other than to cause the prince to sit up even straighter.

After three interminable heartbeats, the dirt directly in front of the horse exploded. Neighing wildly, the animal reared up, throwing the prince off backwards. The Persian leader scrambled to his feet, and caught the reigns before his mount ran off.

"Walk away," Tiny Voice instructed.

Rook needed no urging, and trotted off, around the prince and away from Babylon.

They continued off in a straight line, and the city shrank behind them until it was just a low ridge in the distance. At one point, Rook looked back and saw plumes of smoke rising from the irregular line on the horizon marking the city. "Is Babylon burning?" he said, alarmed.

"No," Tiny Voice replied.

Rook waited for some elaboration, but none came. "Why the fires, then?"

That pause. "They mark an event of some significance."

He waited, but again, no further explanation. "What event?"

"I can't know that, but likely some loss. We must keep going, Rook."

He gazed at the columns of menacing smoke, the twisting, snake-like black coils seeming to rise ever so slowly from this great distance, obviously the products of substantial fires. The scope of the demonstration brought home to Rook the vast size of the city of Babylon, that so much fuel could be consumed for the sole purpose of marking an event.

He wondered what loss could elicit such a display.

"Please, Rook, we must continue."

No resisting a "please." He turned and trudged on.

When they came to a slight hollow cradling a large boulder at the bottom, Tiny Voice told Rook that they'd wait here for nightfall, when the shuttle would return to retrieve him. Exhausted, he lay down in the sliver of shade next to the boulder, and promptly fell asleep.

He woke to darkness, confused. It had been a long time since he'd slept without the guiding force of the brain-hand, and he had no idea at first where he was. He sat up, and his head klunked against something hard. It was the boulder. It all came back to him.

"The shuttle is almost here," Tiny Voice said as Rook stood up, steadying himself against the side of the boulder.

The little creature hovered next to him, a comforting hum in the night, and Rook realized that it must have been that sound that had woken him.

"Please remove the device from your ear, and give it to me," Tiny Voice said.

As the haze of sleep dissipated, a dozen questions fought to be heard, and he shivered as he felt the device pulling itself out on its own. He reached up, and it practically jumped into his fingers. In the thin illumination of ten thousand pinpoints of starlight, he saw Tiny Voice there in front of him. He held out his palm, and his little avian companion slowly lowered until two thin appendages the length of his fingernail reached out from its bottom, grasped the ear-thorn, and Tiny Voice was up and away.

Rook's ear felt cold and empty. "That's it?" he said, feeling a little desolate at the sudden break and departure. There was no way now, of course, for Tiny Voice to reply.

He sat back on the ground, and wrapped his arms around himself against the cold night air of the desert. He heard the hum returning, and a moment later, Tiny Voice was there, floating before him. In the starlight, the blur of its wings seemed faintly iridescent. Rook waited, not sure what to do. A moment later, it flitted away, and the sound of tiny whirring wings disappeared into the night. Rook could only conclude that his companion of the last twenty-four hours had come back to bid him farewell.

He felt a slight bump through his feet and rump, like someone dropping a small stone, and turned to find a dark, indistinct mass a short distance away. As he watched, an oval of light appeared, the doorway into the shuttle.

He stepped through, and Hiding Voice greeted him, "Hello, Rook. Please step against the bed." As the straps grasped his ankles and wrists, and the bed tilted back, Rook thought how Tiny Voice was so much like Hiding Voice. But also, different. It was difficult to describe—sometimes he had the sense that Hiding Voice barely knew he was there.

These musings were swept aside as the brain-hand gently grasped and smothered his conscience.

Chapter 4

"Again," Hiding Voice said.

Rook repeated the word. The language was similar to the Greek he'd learned for the previous Earth visit. In fact, absent comprehension of the words, he wouldn't have known they were different.

It had been thirty days since Hiding Voice pulled him from the second long-sleep. The gap in his life could have been a day, or a year. Like last time, recovery of strength had been a long slog—hours and hours on the exercise steps before he was back to normal, if he even knew what that was anymore—he had a hard time remembering.

"Okay," Hiding Voice said, "next word."

This one was like the sound a crow makes when drawing a dove away from its nest so that its companion can sneak in to steal a chick or two.

"Again," Hiding Voice said, repeating the word.

Upon waking from the sleep cycle, before launching into his daily schedule of exercise, language practice, and eating, Rook replayed in his mind the visit to Earth. One question lingered through the day. "Why did the monitor need to hide in my pocket?" he said.

"Are you referring to the Earth drone?" Hiding Voice said.

"Drone? Is that what it's called?"

"That is a succinct description. Repeat the new word."

He tried, not sure how it was any different than the previous one. "So, why?" he added.

"Why, what, Rook?"

"Why did the drone hide in my pocket?"

"Knowing about the drone would confuse your people, Rook. Let's try the next word."

"But the Persian soldiers saw it. It shot something in front of the prince's horse to scare it."

"That is true, and it was unfortunate. The drone should not have revealed itself."

"It saved my life."

"That is true as well. Please repeat the next word, Rook."

He tried, wondering if this was how mockingbirds feel. *The drone saved my life*, he thought. *And, apparently it should not have.*

No, that couldn't be. Hiding Voice must have meant that the drone should have found some other way to save him.

∞

Rook opened his eyes. What had happened? This was not how he normally woke, where the brain-hand lifted him gently from the place of dreams to the reality of his little white cave painted with realistic scenes of a forest. This time something had jerked him from sleep, like his mother calling him to go for water before the sun even peeked over the horizon.

He sat up, feeling a little disoriented. "Hello?"

Hiding Voice didn't answer. The uneasy feeling of something amiss deepened. "Hello?" he called, louder.

The little room seemed suspended in time. He slid off the bed, and saw why. The forest surrounding him had frozen. Leaves and branches, twisted in the wind, remained precisely in place. A yellow-breasted bird hovered motionless in the air, defying the pull of gravity.

And, something else. He walked over to get a better look. In the middle of the trunk of a large oak was … a hole. As he approached, the contents of the hole shifted, sliding slowly sideways. He stopped dead, staring. The hole wasn't part of the picture, it was in the wall itself. A circular opening the width of his hand had appeared. Through the hole, he was looking at another frozen outdoor scene some paces beyond.

Stepping slowly, cautiously forward, he peered through. He was looking into another room the same as his own. Not quite the same—the scenes shown on the walls were of an open plain of high grass. Lone trees, scattered like moss-covered mushrooms, dotted the grassy savannah. There was a bed in the middle, just like his, and on it lay … what? The prone figure looked like a person, but if it was, the poor soul must have been trapped in a fire, for the skin was burnt black. He gasped and stepped back when the burnt body opened its eyes and sat up. It was a girl! Her dark hair clung close to her head in tight curls—a soft virtual helmet. She seemed to be about his own age judging by her smooth dark skin, and there was a lot of that. Whereas his clothes extended from chin to feet, only her waist and upper thighs were covered. His sense of propriety prevented him from staring at her bare breasts. Her profile, though, was strikingly attractive, high cheekbones and a small nose flaring slightly into small, symmetrical oval openings.

Her head spun suddenly, and she was staring at him, her brow contracted in bewilderment, and then her eyes opened wide with astonishment. Like the images on the walls surrounding them, they both froze, awed, and then, suddenly, Rook was looking at the missing section of the tree trunk as the forest once again came to life, the wind-blown leaves flipping back into place, the yellow-breasted bird flitting away along its original flight path.

He staggered backwards, his head swimming in a swirl of feelings—shock, hope, joy, and … alarm. He sensed that he wasn't supposed to see this. Something had malfunctioned—the frozen forest simulation, the absence of Hiding Voice, and ... for Maker's sake, a *hole* in his wall?

He jumped when Hiding Voice suddenly said, "Rook, are you okay?"

"Uh, yeah. What happened?"

"We had an incident, Rook, but everything is okay now."

He had never thought that their ship could be in any danger, but his reassurance implied otherwise. "An incident?"

"Rook, when traveling at 98 percent the speed of light, colliding with anything—a grain of sand—can produce great damage."

"We almost hit a grain of sand?"

"It's more complicated than that, but everything is okay, now. There's no need for alarm. We are very capable."

It was unusual—unprecedented—for Hiding Voice to be at all defensive. He'd thought of Hiding Voice as god-like, a rival to Maker ... if there was a Maker. This slight relaxation of class stratum, even if only temporary, emboldened him. "How long until the next Earth visit?"

"Sixteen days, Rook. We are nearing your star system, thus the increased possibility of collision hazard."

"Okay. Thanks." *Here goes.* "Um, what's the purpose of this visit?"

"Purpose, Rook?"

The question was not ambiguous. Hiding Voice was normally one step ahead of him. "Well, why am I going down?"

"To ensure wellbeing for your people."

Rook understood that his "people" were now the entire human race. "Right. But, how will I do this? Another golden cup?"

"No, Rook. The cup was specific to that situation."

"I see. So, how, then?"

"How, what, Rook?"

"How will I ensure wellbeing for Earth?"

"By providing new knowledge for your people. Rook, we should practice some language words."

"What kind of knowledge?"

"Useful knowledge, Rook. Repeat this word."

"But, useful in what way?"

"Rook, please repeat this word."

There was the "please." Hiding Voice had apparently recovered from his vulnerable position.

∞

"Prepare for departure," Hiding Voice said without a hint of sarcasm, even though Rook was strapped immobile again.

There had been little time for Rook to scan the faux-forest for more holes into the adjacent room. His life consisted of four activities: sleeping, eating, practicing the new language, and exercise, where he stared at a section of one wall for the sweaty duration. He now regretted asking Hiding Voice to show him examples of new language words, as he'd done when learning Hiding Voice's own language, since now he was obligated to look at the pictures of objects. His eating time was the only opportunity to casually look around at the walls. So far, he'd detected nothing like the previous hole. He wasn't surprised. The serendipitous gift was probably a fluke, a malfunction caused by the near-collision.

He wasn't quite sure why he hadn't asked about the hole. Hiding Voice wasn't in the habit of volunteering information, but having another person, a human person, so close and yet unacknowledged somehow implied a secret.

And now any further scouting would have to wait. He'd been counting the days, and Rook was sure it had only been fourteen, yet Hiding Voice insisted that it was time to leave for Earth. Rook could only conclude that Hiding Voice had kept him asleep for two whole days. Either that, or the sixteen days had been inaccurate. Or a lie.

All the scenarios were unsettling.

The pressing hand—the acceleration—pushed against his chest, and the shuttle was off. Rook knew what to expect this time, and so the trip down from orbit was easier. As with the previous trip, he then had to wait in the shuttle for daylight. When Hiding Voice woke him, the outer door was already open, and Rook breathed deep the overwhelming sensual mix of Earth scents—flowers, moist dirt, and wood smoke.

Rook heard the familiar buzzing, and the miniature, high-pitched Hiding Voice said, "Welcome again to Earth, Rook."

He was lost in the reverie of fragrant sensation, and opened his eyes when the bindings holding his wrists and ankles gave way. The bed lifted, and he stepped out, into the early dawn to find the little drone directly in front of him. "Hold out your palm, Rook," it said.

In the thin light, he saw a small splinter dangling from two tiny appendages under the drone. He recognized the ear-thorn when the drone dropped it into his hand. He shuddered when he felt the little communication device settle itself into place inside his ear canal. He didn't think he'd ever get used to that.

"Follow me," the drone said inside his head.

Rook fell in behind his flying companion, but stopped and turned, curious. The shuttle had already started away. The metallic boulder, smooth and symmetrical, sailed away into the sky, growing smaller and smaller, until, barely ten heartbeats later, it was just a dot disappearing into the clouds.

"Rook, we must go."

He turned and trudged after the little artificial bird. They crossed a meadow flanked by a wall of tall trees on three sides. Wherever they were, it was obviously far from the previous desert. He stumbled, and soon stumbled again. The tall grass kept catching in his sandals. He wondered why anybody would willingly wear these clumsy things. Bare feet would have been so much better, but Hiding Voice had insisted that he keep them on. The pure-white, ankle-length robe was equally awkward—walking through waist-high grass was like struggling against grasping hands.

"Where are we going?" he asked.

"To a city called Aachen, to see the emperor."

Another emperor, he thought. *Why start anywhere but the top?*

Something else occurred to him—the drone had not only replied directly to his question, but had volunteered additional information. Hiding Voice would never do that.

A man-child—snatched while still proving himself a man—who was worthy of seeing an emperor was surely also worthy of more answers. "You said, 'Welcome again to Earth' back there. Are you ... are you the same, uh, drone from my last visit?"

"Yes, Rook."

"I see. But ..."

"What is it, Rook?"

"How long has it been?"

"One thousand, one-hundred, and fifty-two years, Rook."

He'd asked Hiding Voice, and, although the oblique answer had implied a vast span of time, Rook had decided that he'd misinterpreted it. The drone's response was unequivocal, however. "That's ... that's a long, long time."

"It is, Rook."

"But ... it can't be!"

"Why not, Rook?"

"You're over a thousand years old?"

"Over six thousand years, Rook. Remember, it was four thousand years before your first visit. I think I understand your confusion. Rook, we are different from you. Nothing lasts forever, but we can repair things that go wrong with us. In a sense, we could be immortal."

"I see."

"Rook, does this bother you? Does it make you envious?"

"No," he said. He kicked at a free-standing clump of grass and nearly fell when his sandal became tangled again. "Actually, yes. I guess it does bother me."

"It doesn't seem fair, does it?"

"No, it doesn't." He shrugged. "That's just the way it is," he said.

He was going to say that it was just Maker's way.

"That's right, Rook. That's just the way it is."

He walked on, stepping high to keep his sandals free.

"I'm sorry, Rook," the drone said.

He smiled. One thing he was sure of—Hiding Voice would never, ever talk to him like that.

∞

The sun was nearly up when they reached the city outskirts. The walls of the buildings were constructed with wood, presumably from the trees crowding all around. The roofs looked like shaggy, full heads of hair, that Rook realized as they got closer were layers of straw, nearly as thick as the walls were high. It must have rained recently, for the ground all around was mud. No more grass to trip him, but he had to be careful that the clinging, sucking dark goop didn't pull his sandals right off his feet.

Only a few early people were about, dressed in dirty, course-weaved cloth that hung loosely from their shoulders to their knees, where stringy tatters waved like willows in the wind. When any of these scattered citizens saw him in his pristine white robe, they would stare a moment, and then slink back behind a corner, to peek out every few seconds.

Tiny Voice led him to a small corral where he told Rook to pull out one of the fence rails, a thin, straight wood rod, polished from constant rubbing by the goats within. He told Rook to hold the rod upright, and then the little drone settled himself on top. A moment later, the tip of the rod burst with a light so bright, Rook had to divert his eyes. The small group of more adventurous people that had gathered a stone's throw away gasped and scattered as though chased by a cougar.

"Am I supposed to be a god again?" Rook asked as they set off into the maze of thatched hovels.

"Not exactly, Rook," Tiny Voice said. "They think that you are a messenger from their god."

Rook hesitated. Hiding Voice would rebuke him, but he sensed that Tiny Voice would be more tolerant. "One god, like Maker?"

As soon as he said it, Rook realized that Tiny Voice might have no idea what he was talking about.

"Not exactly, Rook. In the pantheon of your original tribe, Maker was the dominant god, but not the only one."

Apparently Hiding Voice and Tiny Voice talked.

"Since your last visit," Tiny Voice said, "a local monotheistic religion has evolved around a martyred disciple who is believed to be the son of the one god, and who was sent to Earth. So, in a sense, this outgrowth of the religion is no longer monotheistic. In fact, scholars struggle with this, and have constructed a rather transparent idea that their god is indeed only one god, but manifests as three equal parts—the original god, who is the father, the martyred son, and a third ill-defined part they call the holy spirit, who serves as a sort of glue to fill the balance. They seem to place an importance on worshiping just one god."

"Is this what I'm *supposed* to be? A messenger from the three god parts?"

"That is what you represent to them."

Rook didn't press it. Whatever he was supposed to be evidently didn't matter.

As they proceeded into the city, people sprinted on ahead of them, and others peered wonderingly from dark doorways. Soon, they were walking through a fluid crowd shielding their eyes from the blinding source, and parting as they approached, only to fill in behind after they passed, so that they became an isolated island floating along a river of ragged, dirty bodies.

The squat, windowless houses gave way to larger, two-story structures, with occasional edifices built with stone walls, and large, rounded wooden doors. Rook stopped short when he suddenly saw ahead of them something even stranger than the Ishtar Gate—a small mountain rising from the very center of this city called Aachen. It was obviously a mountain, and yet it would have had to have been created by Maker himself. Rook couldn't imagine how even the vast armies of Alexander and his conquered Persians together could have chiseled this down from raw mountain bones. It would have taken centuries. If made by men, what purpose could they have imagined in the thin spires reaching toward the clouds and terminating in points as delicate as a feather quill?

"We must keep moving," Tiny Voice said in his ear. The crowd had gathered closer, and pulled back quickly as Rook started forward again.

It wasn't long before he saw the truth, and he stopped short again in amazement. The mountains were actually massive buildings built from large, regular blocks of stone. Rook had difficulty believing his eyes. Who had built these? Why? He wondered if Hiding Voice was jealous.

"They put much effort into glorifying their god," Tiny Voice said, guessing his thoughts. "Rook, we must keep going."

The closer they came, the more imposing the sheer stone cliff faces and spires loomed above them. By the time they reached the bottom of a wide set of steps leading to doors five times the height any man would need, the ragged crowd had been left behind, and a retinue of men dressed in bright colorful robes and flanked by soldiers stood waiting at the top of the stairs.

"Are these priests?" Rook whispered.

"In a way," Tiny Voice replied. "They are actually the emperor's administrators, but this emperor's father aligned the empire so closely with the religion's leader in a nation far to the south, these men could be considered as much representatives of their church as of the government."

One of the officiators, the oldest of the group, made his way down the flight, taking each of the dozen steps carefully, each step a small challenge unto itself. Rook had noticed that Tiny Voice's blinding light had dimmed and disappeared as they approached their destination, and he glanced up to find his companion gone.

"I am still here," Tiny Voice said from somewhere invisible. "Hold your rod against the ground with one hand, and raise the other, and then repeat this," Tiny Voice said.

Their greeter stopped two steps above and, breathing hard, placed his palms flat against each other in front of him, and replied.

"You gave greeting," Tiny Voice explained, "and he returned in kind. He asked whether you come as before. Say this."

Rook repeated the inscrutable words, wondering why the man thought he had been here before.

The wrinkled old face lifted in assumed dignity and spoke.

"You told him that you came to deliver a message to the emperor," Tiny Voice said, "and he told you that the emperor is away, but that he would carry the message to him when he returned. Say this."

Now the old eyes flickered with annoyance, and then his brow contracted.

"You told him that you understand that the emperor would not want to face you—you see, he knows that we know that the emperor is here—and then you delivered the message that the emperor should include his youngest son by Judith in ruling the empire."

The old man nodded, spoke, and turned to make his labored way back up the stairs.

"Say this quickly," Tiny Voice instructed.

The bent man stopped, turned, looked at him a moment, and then motioned for him to follow.

"What did I say?" Rook whispered.

"You told him that you wanted to pay reverence."

Instead of climbing the stairs, the man hobbled off to the side.

"Go with him, and attempt to help him," Tiny Voice said.

Rook hurried to catch up, and took his elbow in support, but the old man shook it off angrily. "You knew that he'd do that?" Rook whispered.

"Yes," Tiny Voice replied. "It serves to emphasize his mortality."

Slowly, agonizingly, they made their way off to a small building, with two guards stepping in to positions on each side. After the bright morning sun, the interior was essentially black, and Rook stepped carefully as he followed his guide into the cool darkness. Small windows provided some light, and as Rook's eyes adjusted, he saw a number of tables. The administrator/priest led them to one on which lay a bundle of clothes, which, as Rook drew near, he saw was actually a body ... and it was wearing the same robe as himself, the dark splotch of blood in the midriff setting a macabre contrast to the pure white cloth. When they finally arrived next to the table, Rook could see that it was a woman, but a woman nearly as strange as the one he'd seen through the hole in his wall. Her face, although relaxed in death, seemed contorted in agony. "Who is she?" Rook whispered.

"An ambassador," Tiny Voice replied, "like you."

"What happened?"

"Her initial contact went awry. There was confusion, a misunderstanding, and one of the guards acted rashly. Rook, place your hands reverently against each side of her head, and hold them there."

Her skin was cold, and, despite the fact that he'd dealt with death within the tribe, he was anxious to get this over with. He nearly jumped away when he felt something wiggling against his palm just as Tiny Voice said, "Rook, take the communicator."

He lifted his hands away, cupping the squirming little worm in his palm.

"You did admirably," Tiny Voice said.

Rook wondered at how his little companion evidently knew that he'd retrieved it, and then guessed that the expatriate ear-thorn had told him.

The world was full of hidden beings talking together without words.

At least, his world was.

Blaine C. Readler

Chapter 5

Rook opened his eyes. "Are we down?" he said.

"Yes, Rook," Hiding Voice replied. "The portal will open soon."

Rook felt as though he was being smothered lying there strapped down on the table. The clothes that he'd donned at Hiding Voice's direction before leaving orbit seemed as heavy and cumbersome as if he'd tied a couple of buffalo hides to his body with twine. The heavy, stiff pants—held up with a leather strap at the waist—made walking seem like wading through thick snow. The shoes were stiff, shiny leather, with a flat bottom, and rounded top. Compared with soft moccasins, these were essentially torture. His shirt attached in the front with little round disks prodded painstakingly through holes barely large enough to take them. Worst of all was a heavy, cumbersome knee-length jacket, again secured with disks-and-holes, that, as far as Rook could tell, served no purpose other than to hide the shape of his body.

He had asked what animal the shoes and pants-strap were made from, and Hiding Voice had replied that there were no animals on the starship. Rook refrained from pointing out that he was an animal, since he'd finally accepted that asking Hiding Voice questions was an invitation to frustration. For example, when he'd asked how long it had been since the last visit, Hiding Voice had replied that it had been eight months. When Rook explained that he'd meant Earth-time, Hiding Voice had said that for him, it had been truly eight months, and then changed the subject. When he'd struggled to don the burdensome clothes, he'd asked why such ridiculous attire, and Hiding Voice had responded that they were appropriate for the current culture on Earth. And when he'd pointed out that the clothes that he'd worn the last two visits were definitely not appropriate for those cultures, Hiding Voice had simply agreed, and, as usual, changed the subject.

He knew better than to ask something so useful as the purpose of this new visit.

The bindings on his wrists and ankles suddenly gave way, the table tilted up, and a black oval opened in the white wall in front of him. "Depart." Hiding Voice said.

Rook knew by now to step carefully, as the shuttle could have landed anywhere—the side of a mountain, the shore of a lake. No dawn this time. The crescent of an old moon hung above the horizon, however, marking an imminent arrival of the sun. Rook relaxed when he heard the welcomed buzz, and a miniature voice said, "Hello, Rook. You can step forward. The grass is moist with dew, so be careful not to slip."

He realized why when he found that the ground sloped down slightly. A short distance away, he saw scattered little squares of light, some close to the ground, and others higher, as though in trees. "Windows," Tiny Voice explained, "lit by lamps that burn oil. Hold out your hand, Rook."

He took the ear-thorn and let it squirm into his ear canal.

"Do you see the two lit windows, one on top the other straight ahead?" Tiny Voice said inside his ear. "Walk towards those."

Details began to form as Rook's eyes adjusted to the darkness, and he could see that he was in a wide meadow, lined on one side by buildings, where the lit windows indicated early risers. The amber light glowed softly on curtains, warm and inviting. As they got closer, he saw that these buildings were constructed entirely from wood, like those in Aachen, except that these were different colors, and the windows were covered by something transparent, like thin sheets of ice. "Glass," Tiny Voice explained, "they make it by heating a special type of sand."

It seemed like just a short time ago that he and Tiny Voice were making their way through an early dawn together. For him, of course, it had only been a matter of a dozen waking weeks. "How long has it been?" Rook asked.

"One thousand, thirty-six years, Rook," Tiny Voice said.

Another thousand, Rook thought. He tried to grasp that, to imagine what it must be like to wait a thousand years for another visit from the starship. He tried, and failed. It was far beyond the reach of his imagination. "Can you tell me what I'm doing this time?" Rook asked.

He'd spent weeks learning to pronounce words of the new language, and this one had been the most difficult so far. Whereas the sentences of the previous two had followed an undulating terrain of excited pitch mixed with sober calm, this new language loped along in a continuous drawl, each word flowing seamlessly into the next.

Tiny Voice didn't answer. He was about to ask again, when he noticed a dark patch of blotted out stars rising swiftly into the air—the shuttle returning to the starship. As it grew smaller and smaller, it suddenly burst with white light, catching the rays of the rising sun high above.

"You are going to talk to an actor," Tiny Voice finally said. Rook sensed that his companion had been waiting to talk. "This country has been waging a civil war for the last four years, and you are going to suggest that he should do what he can to help one side."

"That's all?" Rook said. *They brought me here in a starship to suggest something to someone?*

"This man could play a key role in the struggle."

Rook shrugged. He was just the mouth. The brains had their own logic. "What has happened since my last visit?" he asked.

He didn't expect an actual answer, and was surprised when Tiny Voice replied. "Emperor Louis, the son of Charlemagne, took your advice and included his youngest son in the division of the empire. War subsequently broke out between the siblings, and the empire was essentially disbanded. Rook, it is preferred that you don't ask these questions."

They'd arrived at one of the buildings, and Tiny Voice told him to wait a moment. Rook heard the soft clucking of large birds in a nearby pen, "chickens." Hiding Voice obviously preferred that he didn't ask questions, but he never admitted it like Tiny Voice.

"Rook," Tiny Voice said, "walk quietly between these buildings, and knock on the front door of this one."

He made his way around, and stumbled in the darkness on a loose board of the front steps. He heard voices from within, and the door opened before he even knocked. In the soft glow of lamp light, he faced a short man with tousled hair and an open shirt who said something that sounded like the moan his uncle would make when pushed into the firelight for a story.

"Say this," Tiny Voice instructed.

He tried, mouthing the non-descript words like he might a fistful of boiled grain.

The man looked at him funny, and called over his shoulder. A moment later a taller man appeared, this one groomed and alert. His mustache rounded the corners of his mouth, as though containing it, keeping it apart from his nose.

"Say this," Tiny Voice told Rook in response to the man's question.

The man studied him a moment. He motioned the shorter man back inside, stepped out, and closed the door behind him, leaving them both in near darkness. The conversation bounded along too quickly for Tiny Voice to provide a running side commentary. It was all Rook could do to squeeze out another set of muffle-mouthed words before the man jumped on them, rolling the communication forward, stumbling headlong. At least, this is how it seemed to Rook.

He was beginning to think that his mouth was growing numb from the workout when the man suddenly stopped and placed a hand on his shoulder. Rook felt him take his hand, shake it, and then he opened the door and disappeared inside.

Rook stood staring at the closed door. Something important had apparently happened, and he'd been half of it, and he had no idea whatsoever what it was.

"We need to go," Tiny Voice said.

As they made their way back through the meadow, Rook asked, "What was that all about?"

"You told him that, upon your honor, you represented a neutral faction in the civil war struggle, and that it was your assessment that he had a momentous and historic role to play."

"On my honor?"

"They talk a lot about that in this time period."

"Did I tell him what kind of role he should play?"

As Rook said this, he heard the buzz of Tiny Voice rise up and fade as it rushed away. "Stay where you are, Rook," Tiny Voice said in his ear.

"Where are you going?"

"I must take care of something. Please stay where you are."

As the purring buzz of Tiny Voice disappeared, Rook heard men's voices, shouts and calls. He turned towards the sound, and saw at the far side of the meadow, maybe a dozen houses away, three flames bouncing their way forward along the side of the meadow, away from the houses. He recognized these as torches—he'd carried them himself during the tribal night festivals.

Suddenly, a pure white light appeared ahead of them, this one unwavering, obviously Tiny Voice. The men's shouts swelled as they rushed forward. They ran fast, the torch flames flapping, leaning backwards against the rush of air. Tiny Voice stayed ahead of the men, matching their pace so that he was always seemingly within a few pouncing paces. The mob, shepherded by the alien drone, moved off into the forest.

Something caught Rook's eye. Movement. A shadow, gliding along, angling away from the men in a line that would bring it near him. Blackness along the eastern horizon had given way to the gray preamble of approaching dawn. In the faint light, Rook saw that it was a person, running, staying low, glancing back at the receding men. Folds of clothes undulated in flight, like drying deer hide waving in a stiff breeze. The clothes extended from neck to foot. It dawned on him that it was a dress. He'd seen these in some of the images that Hiding Voice displayed when he was learning to speak this culture's words. The fleeing person was a woman. The outfit included a ruffled head covering, making her look like a wilted daisy.

Why would a mob of men chase a woman? A common practice of rival tribes—including his own—had been to kidnap young women, who would take a mate, and become integrated. Rook wouldn't have thought that a culture so far removed in time would continue the practice. When you lived in one place, in a house, her brothers would know where she was, and come and take her back.

She must have done something wrong. The men wanted to capture, maybe punish, her. Rook's first thought was to intercept and hold her until justice could be brought, but he remembered that Tiny Voice was leading them away. The drone wanted her to escape.

The fleeing woman was close now, but suddenly disappeared. He saw her get up on hands and knees. She'd probably tripped on the ridiculously cumbersome dress. Her head turned towards him, and ... there was no face inside the ruffled boundary. Rather, there was a face, but it was dark. White eyes stared at him.

Tiny Voice had been clear. He wasn't supposed to move. It was such a short distance, though, and Tiny Voice was helping her. He'd *want* Rook to help as well.

He started forward, and the woman scrambled to get up, but tripped again on the dress. He knew she would be wary, maybe frightened of him, so he knelt next to her, trying to appear less threatening.

She said something, a word he recognized, if not understood. It was a word he'd practiced with Hiding Voice, and had spoken more than once with the man with the historic role. Rook couldn't think of anything else, so he repeated it, which he immediately regretted, as it set her off into a bubbling stream of words smeared together to form vaguely defined sentences. She stopped and looked at him.

He shrugged and repeated the word.

She launched again into the stream, her pitch rising in apparent frustration.

He held up his hand and shook his head. Also frustrated, he mumbled, "Take a rest."

That got a reaction. The white eyes opened wide, and blinked. "You're from the ship?"

He sat stunned, as she reached up and brushed his hair back, getting a better look at his face.

It came to him like a blast of winter wind, and he lifted up the ruffled headpiece to reveal a dark carpet. "You're the girl in the next room!"

She smiled. "And you're the boy in the next room."

He lifted his shoulders straight. "You mean man."

Her smile broadened. "And you mean woman."

It was his turn to blink, speechless. A hundred questions crowded together. Instead, he said, "How?"

"How, what?"

"How ... did you get here?"

"The same as you, I imagine. By the shuttle."

"No, I mean *here*, now. Those men," he said, gesturing vaguely off towards the distant shouts.

"My mission went bad."

"Mission?"

"My *mission*. The same reason that you're down here."

"I came down to talk to a man."

"That was it? That was the mission?"

He shrugged. "Yes."

"What did you talk about?"

He shrugged again.

"You weren't able to talk to him?"

"Yes, we talked."

"What about?"

"I don't know."

She opened her mouth, and closed it again. "I think I understand. You don't understand English, do you?"

"English? What's that?"

She sighed. "The language you spoke."

Rook was getting it. "You understand the language?"

"Of course. How could you talk to that man if you don't understand?"

"Tiny Voice—the drone—tells me what to say."

She nodded slowly.

"I can't learn a whole new language every *visit*," he said, irritated. A woman wasn't supposed to best a man. At least not openly.

"What do you do with all your time, then?"

He lifted his shoulders. "Sleep."

Again, she nodded, a knowing agreement.

"It's not my *choice*!" he exclaimed.

"Shh!" she whispered, glancing back towards the forest.

"What was your mission?" he asked quietly.

"I'm supposed to be a freed slave that came north, to the non-slave side. I was supposed to talk to two men about going south—into the slave side—after the war to incite the slaves against their masters. These men are secretly in favor of the slave side, and this is exactly the sort of talk that they fear."

"Slave?"

"Yes, a slave." She looked at him funny. "That's what this war is about."

"The civil war," he said. He hadn't been quite sure what that meant when Tiny Voice told him.

"Yes, of course. This whole country has been consumed by it for years."

"What happened? Why were they chasing you?"

"I guess now that the war is almost over, they're getting desperate, and don't care much whether their true loyalties are revealed."

"What would they have done if they caught you?"

It was her turn to shrug. "Kill me, I supposed. But they'd have to do it out of sight, since this state is technically not part of the south."

"A woman was killed during my last visit," he said, wondering if it was something about being a woman that was so fatal.

She nodded. "It goes with job, I guess."

He looked at her. It was a question he hadn't dared ask Hiding Voice. "What *is* our job?" he said.

She shrugged again. "To perform the missions."

"Yes, I understand that. But what are the missions about?"

She took a breath and let it out slowly. "Amina won't tell me—"

"Amina?"

"The ship. That's what I call her. Queen Aminatu was a powerful African ruler."

"You mean the voice that talks to me?"

"Yes, I guess."

"But it's a man."

"Have you seen this man?"

"Well, no."

"It's not a man at all. It's the ship."

"The ship talks?"

"Yes."

"Who makes it talk?" Rook imagined a man somewhere talking through tubes inside the walls.

"Nobody makes it talk. It thinks for itself."

Rook let it go. He'd have to consider this. A boat that thinks. "Why do you call the ship a queen's name?"

"Well, she rules over everything in her domain. What do you call her?"

Rook hesitated. "Hiding Voice" suddenly seemed naïve. "Silent Bear," he said.

It wasn't a complete lie. He'd often compared Hiding Voice to his reticent uncle. They both answered questions as though it caused pain.

"That's romantic. But I was saying that even though Amina side-steps my questions, I have to believe that the missions are somehow supposed to affect the course of civilizations."

"Why?"

"If I had to guess, maybe to help humans along."

"How do you know so much?"

"I ask questions, I guess."

"I ask questions."

"True. Questions aren't the best path. I read a lot."

"Read?"

"Uh, you don't know how to read?"

"I don't' even know what that is."

She was silent. He could make out her pretty face in the growing dawn light. She looked at him with what he took to be pity. He vowed to learn to do this "reading," whatever it was.

"Hear that?" she said, putting her hand to one ear.

He did. Tiny Voice was returning. "What is your name?" he asked. It suddenly seemed an important point.

"Jamail. What's yours?"

"Rook," he said.

"That's a nice name. It's very good to meet you, Rook," she said holding out her hand.

He shook it. "It is nice to meet you, Jamail."

They both turned as the buzzing became visible as a soft blur against the pre-dawn sky.

"Follow me," Tiny Voice said in Rook's ear.

When he stood up, Jamail said, "Is it taking us to the shuttle?"

"I guess," he said as they set off after the drone. He was determined to find out more about his new world. He was ashamed that Jamail, a woman, was effectively his senior. "That man I talked with," he said.

"Yes, Rook?" Tiny Voice said.

"Who was he?"

"I told you that he is an actor. His name is Booth. John Wilkes Booth."

Blaine C. Readler

Chapter 6

Rook stepped up, stepped up, stepped up. It seemed harder than last time. He'd been awake for eight days, and he still hadn't recovered all his strength. He'd asked Amina—he thought of her that way now rather than Hiding Voice—if it was maybe bad to be sleeping for such long periods, over and over. Her response had been that sleeping was a far better alternative than idling awake for so much time between visits.

Rook noted that his question remained unanswered.

As he stepped and sweated, Rook stared into the fake forest. Two butterflies wandered by. Both had red patterns, and Rook was sure these were the same two he'd seen before. Many times. He couldn't shake the restless unease that had dogged him since waking. The last time he'd seen Jamail had been when they entered the shuttle to return to orbit, and now it felt as though someone had strangled him mid-breath.

Someone had, and that someone was not some one. It was Amina. Every inquiry had been met with first diversion, and then outright refusal, that it was best for him not to worry about Jamail. Amina wouldn't even confirm whether she was still with them.

Rook still didn't quite get that, how a boat that flew between stars could think and talk, but he had to accept it. Somehow, he trusted Jamail. She was a woman, but she was so

… sure of herself. He hadn't doubted her for even a moment during their short time together.

Perhaps as recompense for denying him—or maybe as a diversion—Amina had been teaching him to read. In actuality, Rook had the idea that the ship *wanted* him to learn. Amina said that this cycle had been significantly shorter than the previous, and that, in fact, the language would be the same for this mission. Instead of simply learning to pronounce words, Amina was teaching him to understand. As he learned to speak the language, word-by-word, he learned to read as well. Between the two, he sometimes thought that his brain was going to melt and run out his ears.

A fawn wobbled into the clearing after his mother, the same fawn, and the same mother he'd seen before. Many times.

∞

"Don't open that attachment of the pants, Rook."

Amina had been speaking to him exclusively in the new language—English—for days now, giving him as much practice as possible. He didn't understand what "attachment" meant, but he could guess it was the snap above the zipper. "They are too bite," he said, leaving the pants go, but yanking ineffectively at the taught, course-weaved blue material.

"I think you mean 'tight,' Rook, and that is the style. It is popular now."

"Well, it seems like civilization is going backwards," he grumbled.

His shirt was one piece that he had to pull over his head, and the material was the opposite of the pants, thin and light. It had words on the front that read, "Let's not and say we did!"

"Time to lie back," Amina said.

The straps closed around his wrists and ankles, and the bed tilted back. He looked down and admired his shoes, the one superior aspect of this new outfit. The soles were formed from a soft, yet firm base, and covered in a tight-weaved cloth that embraced his feet comfortably. "You never wait for mine portion," he said.

"You mean, 'my permission,' Rook."

"I will look like idiot."

"You mean, 'like *an* idiot.'"

"Exactly."

Seconds later, he closed his eyes and clenched his jaws through the familiar tumbling and jostling, until the shuttle came to rest ten minutes later. "Minute" was a new English word. A second was one heartbeat, a minute was sixty of those, an hour sixty of those. These people were obsessed with sixty, even though they had ten fingers and toes like everybody else.

The oval portal opened to the darkness of night. "Leave quickly," Amina said.

The straps disappeared, and the tilting bed practically flung him out.

The warm buzz of Tiny Voice welcomed him. "Step away quickly," the high-pitched, nearly comical voice of the drone said.

"What's the rush?" Rook said, stumbling forward in the dark. He noted that Tiny Voice was also using English.

"The shuttle must get away immediately."

"Why?"

"It will have been detected, and people will come to investigate."

"But, it's dark."

"The civilization of this time has developed many uses of electromagnetic energy. In this case, it's called radar."

A new word to remember. "Won't they find me?"

"Yes, if we don't hurry away. Hold out your hand."

Two "minutes" later Tiny Voice spoke inside his head, "Do you see that light on top of a pole?"

Rook realized that he was actually surrounded by distant lights, little lit squares arranged in precise rows and columns, what he took to be windows in buildings. It would have been a lot of torches. Rook had the sense that the little squares of steady, white light were not fire, though. One unwavering light was brighter than the rest, and was clearly closer. "There?" Rook said, pointing.

"Yes, Rook. Make for that light as fast as possible."

The buzz of the drone stayed just ahead of him as he trotted towards the light. The ground was covered in what seemed to be a thick grass, cut short to form a continuous carpet. He could smell the damp greenness of it.

As they approached the light on the high pole, Rook thought that it stood at the edge of a lake, but upon reaching it, he saw that it was not water, but a level, hard surface, made from little pebbles set firmly into something black that bound them together. He tapped at it with his toe, and then stomped. The substance was as hard a rock.

"It's an artificial surface," Tiny Voice said, "called macadam. Rook, lie down on this bench," the drone said, hovering above what was also clearly man-made, a flat surface made of horizontal slabs—what Rook found to be metal—to sit on, with a backrest made of the same thing. Yet another word, "bench."

He lay down on his back, looking up at a handful of stars bright enough to shine through the dim glow of haze.

"Lay on your side, Rook," Tiny Voice said.

"Why?" he asked as he re-positioned himself and bringing his knees up so that he could fit between the armrests on each side.

"You are going to pretend to be asleep."

"Why?"

"Men will arrive shortly to investigate the shuttle that they detected."

"How do you know?"

"They communicate using that same invisible energy, and I can listen."

"And they need to think I'm asleep?"

"They'll think that you are just another person without a house to live in."

Rook didn't understand why the people's families didn't let them in, but he let it go. Tiny Voice would probably use more words that he'd have to try to remember.

"Here they come," Tiny Voice said. "Lie still and be quiet."

He heard the hum of little beating wings fade away, and soon saw blue and red colors through his closed eyelids. He couldn't resist opening his eyes briefly, and saw a car pull up and stop. He recognized it from Amina's lessons. The car had one word painted on the side, "Police." He knew what that meant, and clenched his eyes shut.

He heard a man's voice, laughing about "you eff ohs." Another man said that at least it got them out of the projects for a while, and the first man chuckled and agreed, saying that the only danger here was one homeless drunk.

Rook heard another car stop, and more voices, a woman's among them. The voices moved away, and he risked a peek. Beams of light swung back and forth, probing the area where the shuttle had landed. He could see that the light came from something the police carried in their hands. He closed his eyes, and waited, and eventually the voices returned, car doors slammed, and the sound of engines faded away. He opened his eyes, and he was again alone.

"Okay, Rook," Tiny Voice said in his head, as the buzz of its flight returned, "let's go."

He sat up, feeling stiff from the awkward position. Why would anyone want to sleep on the bench, he wondered, when they could be comfortably sprawled on that short grass? "Where are we going?" he asked, following the drone across the macadam.

"Your mission this time is more involved, Rook. There is a man named Peter who thinks that you have been communicating with him, when, in fact, it was me."

Rook assumed that he must have misheard. "How could anyone confuse me with you? I'm a person, and you're a ..."

"An alien intelligence?"

"Uh, yes."

"Rook, this civilization—your people—have developed what they call technology. They have traveled to the moon, and they build boats that swim under the water for months without surfacing. They travel in cars, as you've seen, and they fly thousands of miles in less than a day in machines that carry them through the air. They can talk and write and read messages at great distances. They don't have to be together. This man, Peter, has never seen me."

Rook was silent, absorbing it all. Could he believe Tiny Voice? Why would the little drone lie? But boats that swim under water? Flying machines that carry people?

On the other hand, he himself flew between stars.

He sighed. "So, what is my mission?"

"You must talk to Peter who thinks that I have been you. You will simply confirm what I have been telling him. It is important that he sees you in person."

"What have you been telling him?"

That slight, palpable pause. "Rook, this is complicated. Peter works at a place where he has access to infrastructure control. I have been helping him understand this better."

"What is infra structure?"

"As I said, Rook, your people have developed complicated machines, and the infrastructure is the technologies that provide support for all the different machines the people use."

"And, he needs to see me."

"Yes, Rook. This is necessary for him to trust you."

"You mean, to trust you."

That odd pause. "Of course, Rook. It is actually me that he will be trusting."

He sighed again. "Won't he be sleeping?"

"It will be dawn soon, and you are going to meet him on his way to work. But first, we must pick up some identification for you."

Rook learned that they had landed in a park in a city, and that a park was an area set aside to remind people what was there before the city was built. Once out of the park, Tiny Voice rose high into the air where others wouldn't hear him. Rook was daunted by the austere, geometrically precise travel avenues—some for cars, some for people—and the sheer, looming, monstrously tall buildings, whose sides were cliff faces higher than any mountain he'd ever seen. Only a few other early morning people made their way hurriedly along the lit people-ways, and they ignored him completely, walking with their eyes fixed on the hard, flat ground directly in front of them, or peering at little glowing tablets held in their hands. Tiny Voice told him to ignore them in turn, to avoid meeting their eyes. When he asked why, Tiny Voice told him that it would make them nervous. Rook didn't want to annoy his guide with too many questions, so he didn't ask what there was about him that people would find so threatening.

The city was built in regular squares, and they walked along three consecutive sides, and then turned left and walked along two more. When they came to a narrow opening between two buildings, as much a cleft in the mountain of buildings as a walkway, they turned in. Somewhere out there, dawn was blossoming, but inside this artificial cavern, only the still-dark sky was visible far above. "There's a door on your left," Tiny voice said. "Knock on it."

As he did, the sound thudded up and down the narrow alley. Rook could tell that the door was made of metal, and he wondered that this civilization would invest so much precious material unnecessarily. Rook waited, and Tiny Voice told him to knock again. A moment later the door flew open, and he was facing a plump, middle-aged woman with tangled gray hair that she brushed out of her face with a quick flick. She wore a one-piece dress made of thin, worn cloth that hung straight down from her shoulders, as though trying to hide the fact that she was large. He was expecting something at least as comely as the dress that Jamail had worn, and wondered if perhaps they'd come to the wrong door, maybe that of a slave.

"Waddaya want?" she said, annoyed.

Rook had no idea what she had just said. "Tell her that you're here to pick up the passport," Tiny Voice said in his ear.

He told her, and she nodded, still scowling. "You must be the Russian."

He stared at her. "Yes," he said, when Tiny Voice prompted him.

She turned and disappeared inside. Rook didn't know if he was supposed to follow her, but he decided that if he had to guess, he'd guess to stay outside. The air wafting from inside smelled bad.

She returned with a small book—Amina had shown him images of books. He reached to take it, and she pulled it back. "Pay first, Rusky," she said, holding out her palm.

"Give her the papers in your right pants pocket," Tiny Voice said.

Rook handed the folded bills to her, and she counted them, licking her thumb as she rifled through. "Not enough," she said, looking up at him. "You owe me another fifty."

"Tell her that this was the agreed price," Tiny Voice said.

She stared at him, and held out the bills. "Sorry," she said. "Gimme the passport."

He reached to take the money, and she snatched it back. "Fine," she growled, reaching to pull the door closed. "Russians are all crooks," was the last words Rook heard before the metal door slammed shut, scaring a small rodent that scampered off into the dark recesses.

Rook slipped the little booklet into his pocket and they set off again. The lights above the streets went off as daylight replaced them. "What's a Russian?" Rook asked.

"A person from another country," Tiny Voice replied.

"A person from any other country?" Rook said, "Or, from a country called Russian?"

He'd been noting that this English language could be ambiguous.

Tiny Voice didn't answer.

"Hello?" Rook said.

Still no answer.

He stopped, and a man bumped into him from behind. "Watch it," the man griped, and walked on without waiting for an apology.

Rook looked up, but the little drone would have been invisible against the gray, overcast sky. "Are you there?" he said, feeling suddenly lost and vulnerable. He had no idea where or when the shuttle would return. He berated himself, and vowed never to let that happen again. Assuming there was an "again."

That's when he noticed somebody else looking up. This man was just inside the building next to him, and turned to look at him, directly into his eyes. Rook froze. It wasn't just that the man was looking at him, it was how intensely he stared, as though as surprised as he was to find them both there.

Then Rook realized that there was a street running through the building, and this didn't make sense. A car drove by behind him, and an identical car drove by inside the building. It came to him that this was a reflection, and the man in the building was actually him. He raised his hand, and his ghost raised his in return. Rook had seen the reflection of his own face in water many times, but never standing upright.

This was the first time he'd ever seen his full profile, and it wasn't too bad—broad shoulders, and firm thighs, clearly defined inside the tight pants.

"Rook," Tiny Voice said, "something is seriously wrong."

Uh, oh. "What?" Rook said. He looked up and down the street, but, although people walked past, nobody paid him any attention.

"We have lost all contact with the ship."

"The starship?"

"Yes, Rook. I have a suspicion, and if true, it is bad indeed. We should proceed quickly to the coffee shop where we will be meeting your contact."

"Uh, okay. Which way?"

"To your right. Walk quickly, but don't run."

Two square sides—two blocks—later, Rook was almost run over by a car, missing him by inches, a horn blaring as it rushed past. Tiny Voice explained that people walking had to wait for an orange hand on the other side to be replaced by a white man. Other than stepping in excrement, he made it to the coffee shop with no further close calls.

Rook opened the door and hesitated. Inside, bright points of light reflected off different surfaces, and the sound of many conversations, shouts of orders, clattering cups, and growling machines was an assault on the very idea of stepping forward. A zinging buzz flashed by his head, and the drone flew up and hovered near the ceiling. Something serious indeed must be happening for Tiny Voice to risk being seen.

Rook stepped inside. "What next?" he said quietly, thinking that people would think his mind troubled if they heard him talking to himself, but then he noticed others doing just that—having animated conversations apparently with themselves.

"Do you see that lit screen at the far end of the room?" Tiny Voice said.

"The one hanging on the wall with the moving images?"

"That's a television, Rook. Ask somebody behind the counter to change the channel to a news station."

Heart pounding, Rook walked past a handful of people to where a man standing behind a counter and wearing a green apron was talking to a woman on Rook's side of the counter. "Could you please change the tev-elisun?" he said.

The worker with the apron frowned and told him that he'd have to wait his turn, but the woman he'd been talking with looked at Rook curiously and said, "Do you mean television?"

Rook felt himself blush. "I think, yes."

She smiled patronizingly. "Where are you from?"

He wasn't ready for that question. "A ship," he said simply.

"New to America?"

He paused and nodded. He didn't know what America was, and took a chance.

The response seemed to be the right one. "What country?"

He knew what a country was, and decided to go with the word for his tribe in his own language.

Her brow furrowed. "Is that in Asia? Maybe near Kazakhstan?"

He went with what worked before and nodded.

That seemed to satisfy her, and she turned to the man behind the counter, "Paul why don't you change the channel for him?" She looked back at Rook. "What channel?"

He stared at her. "News," Tiny Voice said, and Rook repeated it.

"Any news?" she asked.

He nodded.

Paul was gesturing impatiently at the line of people waiting.

"Oh, it'll take just a second," the woman said.

Paul sighed, walked to the far end of the counter, and then back. The woman stepped out of line, and pulled Rook with her. They both watched the television screen. Others saw them, and fell silent as they too turned to look. Soon the conversations fell silent one-by-one, and Paul turned up the sound. A serious man was explaining that the Pentagon was making no statements, but that the president had called it the most momentous event in human history, and there was no reason to think that the aliens, if that's what they were, were dangerous.

The room erupted with excited jabbering, and Paul yelled for quiet. The man on the television was saying that the leak had come from within Strategic Command, and that their Space Surveillance Network had picked up the object in geostationary orbit. He seemed unsure of what that was, but explained that the object remained in one spot in the sky—right over Ecuador, the same longitude as Washington DC. The man placed his finger over his ear a moment, and announced that new information had just come in. The alien object was estimated to be at least as large as an aircraft carrier, and probably the size of a mountain. A small object that had landed nearby, here in the city, was believed to have come from this massive intruder.

At this, the room burst again with excited babbling, and Tiny Voice told Rook to step away, to sit at a small table next to the door. This half of the coffee shop was empty, as the rest had jammed in close to the television. "What does it mean?" Rook asked.

"I fear that it means that the starship has been disabled, Rook," Tiny Voice said. "It has lost its ability to hide from radar. Since I am not able to contact the ship, we must assume that it is completely inoperable."

"What happened to it?"

"I have a theory, but it is too complicated to explain now."

"What do we do?"

"All we can do is wait."

"I see. Uh, what about the mission?"

"Perhaps we should try to connect with Jamail so that we are all together."

Rook's ears perked up at that. "She's here? On Earth?"

"Yes. Twelve blocks away."

"We should go there——!"

"Rook, do you see that man that just walked in?"

He did. It was the only other person at his end of the shop, a small man with thin red hair, and a short-cropped beard.

"That is Peter, the one we came to meet, Rook."

"Uh, I thought the mission was called off."

"Possibly. Perhaps we should follow through for now. Maybe you should get his attention, and ask him to sit down."

Tiny Voice had always been decisive, never a "possibly," or a "maybe." Rook found a pliable Tiny Voice a little disconcerting. He caught the man's eyes, and pointed at the chair next to him. Peter glanced around, walked over, and sat down—not in the chair next to Rook, but on the opposite side of the table. He leaned forward on his elbows and said, "What's your name?"

Rook didn't like his eyes. They seemed to crouch behind disapproval. "Stewart," he said, mimicking Tiny Voice's prompt.

Peter nodded. "Were you followed?"

Rook frowned. How would he know? "No," Tiny Voice said urgently.

Peter nodded again. His eyes narrowed. "Where are you from?"

He remembered. "Russia," he said, and then followed with "Saint Petersburg" from Tiny Voice.

"Say only what I say," Tiny Voice told him.

Peter glanced around again, and leaned in closer. "You held back, didn't you?"

Rook stared at him, waiting for a response from Tiny Voice. "What do you mean?" he repeated.

"I think you know exactly what I mean. Your handlers in Moscow told you to give me just a piece, didn't they?"

Pause. "No."

"You think I'm an idiot? Cutting out just DC wouldn't have done anything."

Pause. "Then you probably shouldn't do it," Rook said, repeating Tiny Voice's response.

Peter sat back and eyed him with a smirk. "You thought you could play me. I get it." He nodded knowingly. "I figured it out, though. I figured it *all* out."

Rook stared at him. No response came from Tiny Voice.

Peter's eyes flashed with excitement and he went on. "In ten minutes, the entire north American grid goes down."

Even though Rook understood the language, Peter might as well have been speaking Greek. "That would be a mistake," Rook repeated. It might have been his imagination, but he thought Tiny Voice sounded alarmed.

"For you, maybe. Maybe for your bosses in Moscow. They're not expecting this, are they?" Invigorated by his glee, he didn't wait for an answer. He leaned in again and his eyes bore into Rook's skull. "Do you know what else is carried across the grid fiber?" His voice dropped to a whisper. "Secure FBI communications."

Peter sat back, and his eyes widened in anticipation, and then grew angry when Rook just sat there waiting for some response from Tiny Voice that didn't come. "I can direct the FBI!" he exclaimed, and then glanced around and ducked his head back down. "Don't you see?"

Tiny Voice was silent, and Rook shook his head. That much was true.

"You Russians have no imagination." He looked at his watch. "In seven minutes, instructions will go out to all the FBI field offices to make a series of arrests. Can you guess who are on the lists?"

Rook shook his head. He decided he would do this for all the questions.

"Black leaders," Peter hissed, and his eyes went wide with excitement again. "Can you imagine? All the field offices receive these urgent instructions to make arrests, and then all the power goes down. They have no way to confirm or disprove the orders! They'll have no choice but to make the arrests! In the chaos of grid failure, wild rumors will fly about black leaders being rounded up. Black communities all across the country—Atlanta, Baltimore, Philadelphia, Chicago—will riot. It will prove once and for all that blacks can't be a responsible player in a democracy."

Rook stared at him, hoping that he'd ask a question so that he could shake his head. But Peter just returned his stare. He pulled his hands from the table, and put them in his pants pockets. "You don't care, do you?"

Finally. Rook shook his head.

Peter tsk-tsk'd dismissively. "Of *course,* you don't. It's not your country. You've taken care of your problem. Chechnya's under your thumb."

He stood up and dramatically pushed his chair away. "Get ready to be bowled over," he said, and walked out.

"Rook," Tiny Voice said, "we must hurry to find Jamail."

"What was that all about?"

"I'll try to explain along the way, Rook. Maybe you should run."

"Okay," he said, jumping up and dashing out onto the sidewalk. "Which way?" he asked.

"Rook, let me out."

He'd forgotten that the drone had come inside with him. He opened the door, and the little alien flew out and away down the street. Rook ran after it as Tiny Voice explained about the power grid, and the simmering race tensions that had never been completely resolved since the last time Rook had been here more than a century and a half before. "He was only supposed to bring down the power in the country's capital city," Tiny Voice explained, "and that would have lasted only a short while. This could be quite a disaster."

"Why does he want to make the descendants of the slaves angry?" Rook said, breathing hard.

"He's afraid of them. He thinks that this country should be reserved for just his own ancestors. He belongs to a small group of people called white nationalists. He wants to create as much trouble as possible between his ancestors and theirs. He thinks his ancestors will win, since they've been controlling the country for over two hundred years."

"What was Jamail's role going to be?"

"Rook, she has already informed the FBI about you."

"What?"

"Rook, the main point of the mission was that you be arrested for spying and attempted terrorism."

He stopped short, and the drone circled back. "We must keep going, Rook," Tiny Voice said.

"I was supposed to be *arrested*? That was the *point*?"

"Rook, you are a pawn in a metaphorical version of a chess game."

"I ... I still don't understand. What good would it do to have me arrested—?"

"It would be the next step in destabilizing your civilization."

Rook watched as the drone flew away along the sidewalk. He ran after it.

He had no choice.

Chapter 7

Rook stopped when he came to the curb, glad for the chance to catch his breath. Despite tedious hours on the step machine, he wasn't even close to the body that he'd had when the alien ship picked him up. Then, he could have run for hours wearing down a wounded deer.

"Rook, we must keep going," Tiny Voice said from somewhere above.

"There's no white man," he said, pointing across the intersection.

"That doesn't matter now. All the cars are stopped."

The cars had been moving and stopping in seemingly random patterns and Rook hadn't noticed that now they were all motionless. The ever-present blaring of angry horns had risen to a steady wail. "I can't get across!" he exclaimed. The cars were jammed together, front to back, with no room between.

"Rook ..." Tiny Voice said.

He looked up, but the drone was not visible.

"You are correct," Tiny Voice finally said. "The cars are jammed to the end of the block. You will have to go over."

"What do you mean?"

"Over the cars. Hurry, Rook."

A crowd of people had gathered at the intersection, stymied as well. He took a step back, and his heel landed on something soft. A man behind him yelled and gave him a push. Rook went with the momentum, and scrambled onto the hood of the car in front of him. A horn under him burst to life, and a woman inside the car screamed curses through her open window as he leaped onto the next car. As he jumped from car to car, a cacophony of sustained car horns swelled from below. People, faces twisted in rage, tried to get out of their cars, struggling through the narrow door openings. As he jumped down from the last car, an ear-piercing bang sounded behind him, and something whizzed past his ear.

"Run, Rook!" Tiny Voice implored.

Whatever that bang was, it must have been dangerous.

Rook ran. He needed no urging. At the next intersection, a man in a blue uniform was standing in the intersection, holding his hands out. Whoever he was, the people in the cars obeyed and stayed back. A stream of people walked through the intersection past the obliging man, and Rook ran through as well, pushing people aside to get past. "Hey!" the blue man yelled. "Slow down, buddy!"

Rook ran on, not even looking back. Two cars had crashed together inside the next intersection, and Rook sped past two men yelling and pushing each other's chests. "These people are crazy!" Rook said as he sprinted along.

"This is not normal, Rook," Tiny Voice said. "The power has gone away, and the city needs this to function. This is something that most of these people have never experienced before. Rook, the next building on your left is the FBI office."

"Jamail is here?"

"If she hasn't left already ... correction, she is here."

"You know this?"

"I have detected one of my kind with her."

A flight of six wide steps led up to glass doors. Two men in suits burst through, and trotted down the steps and away along the sidewalk. "They're off to arrest one of the black leaders," Tiny Voice said.

"How do you know?"

"The telephone system has gone down along with the power grid, and they're using handheld communication devices—walkie-talkies. I can hear them talking."

"The invisible energy—radio waves," Rook guessed.

"Yes, that's correct."

"What do we do?"

"I was expecting Jamail to leave the building, but she's still with one of the FBI agents."

"Do we wait?"

"I should be able to talk to her device, but it is uncommunicative."

"This is another voice, like you?"

"Yes—I've picked up more agent conversations. They've decided to hold Jamail, since she's a descendant of the slave race. They're suspicious of her."

"So ... we wait?"

"I don't think so, Rook. They will lock her in a holding place from which she can't leave. She needs to get away before that happens."

"What can we do?"

"You must go in and get her."

"*I* have to get her?"

"No. Sorry, Rook. *We* have to go in together."

He started for the steps.

"Rook, we need a plan," Tiny Voice said.

"Right. Okay," he said, feeling juiced, while at the same time disoriented.

There followed a lot of words whose meanings he had to guess, but Tiny Voice was in a hurry, and Rook got the general gist. He guessed.

Rook ran up the steps, pulled opened the door, and watched as the drone zipped inside.

"What was that?"

A man in a suit stood just beyond the doors watching the little alien hovering high up in the entrance atrium.

"Uh, it's dragging a fly," Rook said, wondering why Tiny Voice was having him say this.

The man looked at him oddly.

"No," Tiny Voice said, "it is a *dragon*-fly."

Rook corrected himself, and the man glanced at his watch, shook his head, and hurried off.

Comfortable sofas clustered around small tables covered in thin books. "Nobody's here," Rook said, gazing around the empty open space.

"This is just the waiting area, Rook," Tiny Voice said. "Jamail's on the third floor. We must go up, through the security check, the metal frame straight ahead."

Rook trotted towards it, but was intercepted by another man, this one in a uniform similar to the man that had been holding off the cars. "Sorry," the man said, holding out his palm, "no admittance until the power's back."

"Tell him this," Tiny Voice said.

Rook listened, and then pointed and said, "I think that's some kind of spy device. Maybe Chinese?"

The drone swooped down from the heights, and hovered just out of arm's reach of the guard who stood staring, wide-eyed. "What *is* it?"

"A spy drone," Rook said, "obviously."

Keeping his eyes glued to the flying alien, the guard stepped slowly towards his desk, but the drone swung around and headed him off, this time coming in close to the man's face, forcing him to lean back.

"Now, Rook," Tiny Voice said in his ear.

"Now, what?"

"The plan, Rook. Run through the security gate."

He did, wondering what else in the plan he'd missed. The guard yelled, and started after him, but the drone headed him off, harassing him, forcing him to stop and swat ineffectively. Once through the metal frame of the security gate, Rook stopped short. There were multiple doors. *Stairs.* He saw the sign, and sprinted for the door. At least he remembered that much of the plan. Beyond it, he started up an endlessly high little room that contained nothing *but* stairs.

"Rook!" Tiny Voice called.

Bear scat! He wasn't used to doors. They were always getting in the way. He turned and flew back down, three steps at a time. "Sorry!" he said opening the door.

The drone buzzed through, and the guard was right behind. Rook slammed the door shut. He felt it knock against something, and heard the guard moan. The drone was waiting at a turn in the stairs, and Rook ran up after him. They passed a door painted with a large number "1," and another with "2" when he heard the door below open, and the guard call out, and then the thumping of his feet up the stairs. The drone waited above "3," and Rook let them both through.

The door opened to a large area. A maze of shoulder high walls filled the space and Rook could tell that these were places where people sat and worked. Nobody was working now. They stood around in groups talking. One woman in a suit looked at him, and walked over. Tiny Voice told him to ignore her, and he pushed past. At this, several men came towards him, but the drone circled around and weaved back and forth in front of their faces. "Spy drone!" Rook called out. Tiny Voice directed him to the back, and through yet another door into a small room with a table and four chairs. A man in a suit sat at one chair, and turned when the door opened. Across from him was Jamail, and she jumped up with a look of shocked surprise. "What are you doing here?" she said.

Loud voices approached outside, and Rook heard a sharp crackling zap, followed by shouts of alarm. He pulled the door shut.

The man sitting across from Jamail—obviously the FBI agent—watched him warily. "Stanislav," he said, pulling a metal tool from a holster inside his coat. "Well, well, you've come to give yourself up?" He glanced at Jamail. "That's him, right?"

She hesitated, weighing the situation, and then nodded. "Yes, that's him."

Rook ignored him. "We have to go," he said to Jamail.

She shook her head, struggling to understand. "Why are you here?"

"The mission is over. The starship is disabled."

She glanced at a round device strapped to her wrist. "Is this true?" she said. She looked up at Rook with concern.

"Is this some kind of code?" the agent asked, glancing at Jamail.

Rook turned to him. "The orders to arrest the slave descendants are false."

The agent watched Rook, keeping the metal tool pointed at his chest. "How did you do it? How many cities did you bring down?"

Rook sighed. "All of them, I guess. Come on, Jamail. We have to go."

She was looking at the device on her wrist, and seemed to be listening. She looked up at Rook and shook her head.

"Tiny Voice—the drone—is waiting outside. Jamail, we came to get you."

She looked at the agent, and back at him, clearly conflicted.

Rook walked over and took her by the arm, urging her to stand up. "This FBI agent plans on keeping you here because you are a descendent of slaves and he's suspicious of you."

The agent stood up abruptly, forcing his chair back with a clatter. His brow had contracted into a threatening frown. "Sit down, both of you," he ordered, holding the tool out with both hands.

"Come on," Rook said, moving towards the door. Jamail came along reluctantly.

When he put his hand on the doorknob, the agent yelled, "Stop! Stanislav, if you try to leave, I will shoot you. Believe me."

Rook turned the knob and opened the door.

"I mean it, damn it!" the agent yelled.

Tiny Voice zipped in and hovered above Rook.

"What the——?" the agent started to say, but a pale flash of light splashed across his chest, and he sat back into his chair, blinking.

"Run!" Tiny Voice said in Rook's ear.

Still holding Jamail's wrist, Rook stepped out into the large room and found a crowd blocking his way. Tiny Voice zipped out, placing himself in front of Rook, and the agent's co-workers stepped out of the way, wary of the alien drone. At the entrance to the stairs, they found the guard blocking the door, pointing the same tool at them. A nasty red welt sat squarely in the center of his forehead. "Sit down on the floor," the guard said. He sounded quite angry.

Rook assumed that they were going to ignore him, as they had done with the others, and he continued on. The guard's eyes flashed with even more anger, and he swung the tool at Rook. "I'll shoot!" the man yelled. "Don't tempt me!"

Rook knew the word "shoot," and he stopped. The man had no spear, sword, or bow and arrow, however, and he was going to start forward again, when Jamail grabbed his shoulder and said, "Stay back."

He still didn't understand what the danger was, but he guessed that Jamail must know. "Tiny Voice can zap him," he said.

"No, I can't," Tiny Voice said. "I must recharge first."

Jamail was watching the drone hovering above them. "Well?" she said.

"Uh, he said that he can't."

"Oh, verdampt!" she muttered, and started forward.

The guard took a step back, and held the tool in both hands. "I'll shoot!" he cried. "I swear!"

"No, you won't," Jamail said, as she reached him. She pushed his hands aside, and with one swift motion, planted her fist in his stomach.

The guard's mouth formed the shape of an "o," and made a sound like wind rushing through pine boughs, and he fell to his knees as Jamail pulled the tool from his hands. The man fell over on his side, pulling his knees to his chest as Rook ran past him, following Jamail and Tiny Voice through the stairway door.

They made it down the stairs and out of the building with no further resistance. Once on the sidewalk, Tiny Voice flew off down the sidewalk, saying, "This way."

Rook ran after him, but stopped and turned. Jamail stood at the bottom of the entrance stairs. "I want some answers!" she called.

"She will have them once we get away," Tiny Voice said.

She stood looking at Rook, apparently oblivious to Tiny Voice. "He said okay, but we have to get away first."

"Who said?"

"Tiny Voice—the drone!"

The glass doors flew open, and three men streamed out. Jamail shook her head, and ran. Rook turned and ran as well as Tiny Voice flew over his head, returning to hold off their pursuers.

"Is Amina—the starship—really disabled?" Jamail said, suddenly running right next to him.

"Yes," Rook said.

"How do you know?"

"Tiny Voice told me."

"And you believe it?"

"Sure." *Why wouldn't he?*

"Why has the power gone down all over?"

"Peter did it on his own. He's a white nationalist. He wants to make a war between white people and slave descendants. Do you know who Peter is?"

"Of course. That explains the chatter about arresting blacks. He faked those orders?"

"Peter talked about 'blacks.' Are they the same as the slave descendants?"

She glanced at him. "What have you been *doing* on the ship?"

"Eating. Sleeping. Exercising."

She shook her head in apparent disdain.

"Turn right," Tiny Voice said in his ear.

They'd come to an intersection, and Rook spun off down the sidewalk in that direction.

"We're going this way?" Jamail called, running after him.

"That's what Tiny Voice said."

"It would be nice to keep me informed," she said, catching up with him again.

"Cross the street," Tiny Voice said.

Cars jammed the intersection ahead, but here the street was clear, and they sprinted across, and then around the next corner to the left, and finally another left into an alley. They sat on the curb, hidden behind a large metal cubic box that smelled of day-old rabbit entrails. Tiny Voice arrived, and positioned himself ten feet up, keeping watch.

"Answers," Jamail said.

"What do you want to know?" Rook said, relaying Tiny Voice's response.

"Why did the drone—Tiny Voice—reveal itself? That's supposed to never happen."

Rook listened to Tiny Voice, and said, "He wants you to take the watch off." He didn't know what a watch was, but decided to be patient.

"Why?" she asked.

"He says that he'll explain soon."

She pursed her lips, and then shook her head. "No."

"He's asking how cooperative it has been—Jamail, what is this 'watch'?"

In answer, she held up her wrist with the strapped-on device. "It's my equivalent of your drone, but it's not very communicative now. It wanted me to sit there in the room until Amina re-activated. It now wants me to sit right here until the starship reactivates."

"It knows that the starship will reactivate?"

"I think it just assumes that."

"Tiny Voice says that it would have caused you to be sent to prison," Rook said. "He wants you to take it off."

"I'm supposed to believe your drone over my guide?"

Rook grasped her wrist. "Tiny Voice says I should take it."

She jerked it away, jumped up, and pointed the tool that she took from the guard at him. "Don't try that again," she warned.

Rook stared at the tool. He was looking into a cylinder the length of his finger. "What is that?" he asked.

"You don't know what a *gun* is? Ho, boy. I thought you were just stupidly brave. Do you know that you came within a hair of being killed back there? Twice."

He remembered the explosive bang when he ran over the cars and the thing whizzing past his ear. He guessed that was a gun as well. This was a very strange world. He decided that he'd have to be more careful.

"I don't understand your drone," she said, sitting back down out of Rook's reach.

"What do you mean?"

"It was so ... obvious. It's supposed to stay hidden, particularly now."

"Why now?"

"The people of Earth have developed technology to the point where they will understand that the drone is not sent by an angel or god. They'll know that it is artificial, made by some intelligence."

Rook listened to Tiny Voice. "He says he can explain, but you have to take off the watch."

She shook her head adamantly. "It's my connection to Amina—the ship. How can I be sure your drone hasn't, I don't know, gone crazy or something?"

"You said yourself that your watch hasn't been very communicative. It wanted you to stay in that room, and Tiny Voice said that they were going to put you some place where you couldn't leave."

"That's what your drone *says*. You're asking me to believe it." She thought a moment. "But, honestly? After those orders came in to arrest black leaders, I suspected I was in trouble."

"See? Also, remember that Tiny Voice saved you during the last visit."

She grinned, ruefully. "When I was an escaped slave."

"It was his idea to get here as fast as we could to save you. He practically got me killed along the way."

She nodded slowly, staring at the ground. She suddenly glanced at her watch. "It's still telling me to stay here until the ship reactivates. It's like it's stuck."

"What if it is stuck, Jamail?" Rook said. "The FBI people are going to be after you, and Tiny Voice has a plan."

He was guessing at that. Tiny Voice seemed to know what it was doing. He glanced up at the drone floating there above the smelly giant metal box. He realized that he'd been blabbing away without instruction from his guide. "You're doing fine, Rook," Tiny Voice said, as though knowing what he was thinking.

He looked at Jamail. She was watching him, waiting. It seemed to him that she wanted to be convinced.

"Ask about her role with the FBI," Tiny Voice suggested.

"You were talking to the FBI to get me arrested," Rook said.

Her brow furrowed. "Yes, but ..."

"What kind of plan was that?"

"Russia is a threat. The country needs to be ready. You were going to be an example of cyber terrorism—look, I specifically asked about your welfare. Amina told me not to worry—that you'd be taken care of, that it would take a while, but you'd be set free ... what's wrong?"

Rook had looked away, up at the drone. "Hold on, Tiny Voice is explaining. Um, he says that the starship had no intention of coming to my aid. When your watch told you that I'd be taken care of, it meant that I'd be taken care of in the government's jail system. I'd be eventually set free, but only after my punishment time was over, probably many years."

She stared at him, her brow seemingly frozen in doubt or concern.

Rook had an idea. "Ask your watch. Ask it if that is the truth."

She shrugged. "Well?" she said, looking at it. "Is Rook telling the truth?"

She listened. "It simply repeats that you were going to be taken care of." To the watch, she said, "Was the plan that Rook would go to jail for many years?"

She waited. "Well?"

She looked up at Rook, her brow now arched above wide eyes. She looked at her watch, and then took it off, and handed it to Rook.

"Smash it, Rook," Tiny Voice said.

"What?" he said, surprised.

"Lay it on the pavement and smash it with that brick next to the refuse bin."

He glanced at Jamail, and reached for the brick.

"What are you doing?" she asked.

He looked at her. The watch was her lifeline to the ship. Tiny Voice was asking him to banish her, to force her to rely on him from now on. He shook his head and placed the watch on the ground. As he lifted the brick, Jamail exclaimed, "No!"

She was pointing the gun at him, the tool that he now knew was lethal. She held it with one hand, the other hand covering her ear, as though containing some turmoil.

"Do it, Rook," Tiny Voice said.

He hesitated. Who did he trust? He closed his eyes, and brought the brick down. A thud, accompanied by a cracking sound, followed. He opened his eyes. Jamail was still holding the gun, but she apparently hadn't fired. He lifted the brick to reveal that the watch was intact, although cracked.

"It's warning that this will have dangerous consequences," Jamail said, darkly, but she let the gun drop.

Rook lifted the brick, and this time brought it down with force, and he heard the watch shatter. When he lifted the brick, the pieces were hardly recognizable. As he watched, they seemed to melt, leaving behind a dozen little pebbles that quickly turned black.

He and Jamail sat staring at the remnants. "Your Tiny Voice better have a good explanation," she said.

Rook nodded slowly. "He says that he can now speak freely."

"Why now?"

"If the starship suddenly reactivated, the watch would have communicated what had transpired."

"So?"

"So, Tiny Voice doesn't want the starship to know what he's about to say."

"Seriously? We destroyed my contact with Amina so that your Tiny Voice could say something?"

Rook shrugged. "He says it's important." He looked at her with alarm. "He says the fate of the Earth is at stake!"

"Well, this should be interesting," she said.

"He's reminding me that having me arrested would destabilize this civilization ... no, he corrected that—having me arrested was just the next step."

"He says that's been the plan?"

Rook nodded. "From the beginning."

Her brow scrunched in thought. "What was your first visit to Earth?"

"Babylon. I gave a golden cup to a general named Alexander."

She nodded. "Alexander the Great. What next?"

"Emperor Louis. He was the son of Charlemagne."

"What happened?"

He shrugged. I—Tiny Voice—advised him to include his youngest son in the division of the empire."

"Next?"

"Hmm, that's when I met you. I talked to a man named Booth."

Jamail's eyes flashed. "John Wilkes Booth?"

"Yes. You know of him?"

She stared at the wall on the opposite side of the alley, then looked at him. "I think your Tiny Voice may be right," she said, seeming amazed at her own words. "Ask it what was special about the cup you gave Alexander the Great."

Before he could say anything, Tiny Voice said, "It was coated with poison that dissolved in alcohol."

Rook blinked. "The fires and smoke after we left! Tiny Voice said that it marked an event of some significance, probably some loss. Maker!" he exclaimed, putting his hands to the sides of his face. "I killed that general?"

"You didn't know, remember?" Jamail said gently. "Rook, the youngest son of Charlemagne wasn't considered a legitimate heir by his half-brothers. Including him in the division of the empire caused civil war. The Empire fell apart. Don't you see? That's what it was all about—breaking up empires. Alexander the Great died suddenly without establishing an heir, and his empire also collapsed because of it."

Rook remembered that Tiny Voice had told him that an empire was like a collection of multiple tribes, but he guessed that this analogy fell far short of the true scope. "What about Booth?"

"Rook, John Wilkes Booth assassinated the leader of that country, the same country we're in now. A great civil war had just ended, and the leader's side had won. This leader, however, was planning on uniting both sides, rather than punishing the other side. After his death, factions of his side did just that—punished the other side, so that the country took a long time to recover. If that hadn't happened, the united country might have been the beginning of the next empire of Earth."

Rook dreaded what he was about to ask. "Did I tell him to kill the leader?"

"Rook," Tiny Voice said, "as Jamail pointed out, you didn't know what you were saying."

"So, I did? I told him to kill the leader?"

"Yes, Rook. You encouraged him."

Rook felt slightly sick, like he might if he'd impaled a cougar with his spear, only to find that, in his haste, he'd killed his brother instead.

"I can see why he didn't want Amina to hear this," he heard Jamail say. "Why is he telling us this?"

"Rook," Tiny Voice said, "I hear the FBI conversations on their walkie-talkies. They've made the connection between me and the disabled starship. They're searching for us in earnest. We must move. Quickly!"

Rook jumped up and pulled Jamail along with him. "We have to run!" he said.

"What's the rush?" she said.

"Tiny Voice sounds alarmed."

"So?"

"I've never heard him sound alarmed."

"Right," she said, sprinting after him down the alley.

They came out on a street jammed with cars and people standing around talking. Tiny Voice directed them around the next corner, and into another alley, where Rook stopped short, and then stumbled forward as Jamail ran into him. Before them crouched something that Rook had never seen before, what at first he took to be a bobcat, but larger. It wasn't a bobcat. Not by any stretch of the imagination. Where a bobcat sat on its haunches with its front paws on the ground, this animal sat firmly back on its butt, freeing the forelimbs to work at something held before a fur-covered face. The paws manipulating the small device were essentially hands covered with what looked like severed bear claws, as though the animal was trying to hide its nimble digits. When Rook and Jamail stumbled to a stop, the animal looked up with eyes that Rook would have sworn were human in their perception and understanding. The beast quickly tucked the device into a halter strapped around both shoulders, and stood up on all fours, whereupon Rook saw that the delicate fingers folded neatly beneath the animal's functional claws, rendering it not some clever new species of monkey, but an adroit predator. The eyes pierced them with a scrutiny that sent goosebumps up Rook's arm and neck. "What is it?" he whispered.

"I have no idea," Jamail said.

"For Maker's sake, Rook, run!" Tiny Voice exclaimed.

He didn't wait, but grabbed Jamail's arm, turned, and pulled them back out of the alley. "Come on!" he cried, and they ran around the next corner. He peeked back, but the beast hadn't followed.

"Do you know what that was?" he asked the drone, hovering just beyond the corner to keep a lookout.

"That is a member of an alien race," he replied. "They are enemies of the starship, and it is they who have disabled it."

Chapter 8

"You said, 'For Maker's sake,'" Rook whispered.

"It was an effective way to communicate the urgency," Tiny Voice said.

They had moved a few blocks farther away, and were hiding in the lobby of an apartment building. Rook and Jamail sat on a bench inside the small area, while the drone had settled to the floor behind them, out of view. A stream of people came and went in front of them. Those arriving punched the dark elevator button a few times before grumbling, or cursing, as they opened the door to the stairs. Disagreements were common among many of those that passed through in pairs, with one side adamantly insisting they heard the news about an alien spaceship, and the other poo-pooing it as just a rumor spawned from the chaos of the power outage.

"Where did it come from?" Rook whispered. He glanced at Jamail. "I'm talking to Tiny Voice."

"A star system far away. About six hundred lightyears."

"No, I mean how did it get there, in the alley? It's either quite a coincidence that we happened to be in the same place, or—" he gulped "—or there's thousands of them."

"There's probably more than one, but surely not thousands. I believe that they've been here in orbit for some time waiting for our next starship to arrive. They would have tracked our shuttle down. They knew we'd be in the city, somewhere close by."

"I didn't know the starship had enemies."

"The two civilizations have been adversaries for a very long time."

"Star wars."

"Not so much a war as mutual containment. Interstellar travel is so tenuous, so time-stretched, that warfare as your people know it is just not possible. When expanding civilizations make contact, a boundary is generally established by default. Whoever arrives first at a colonizable system usually has priority. When conflict does arise, the struggle is contained to the contested star system."

"Earth is a contested planet?"

"Apparently."

"Apparently?"

"I didn't suspect they had arrived until the starship was disabled."

"Rook," Jamail said, breaking him from the conversation inside his head. "What the hell is going on? Earth is in the middle of a star war? There's thousands of those ... things?"

"No. Well, yes." He related the conversation.

"It actually referred to Earth as a colonizable planet?" she said.

"Not directly. Well, yes, I guess so."

She nodded slowly, her mouth screwed tight. "It makes sense," she muttered.

"It does?"

She said something he didn't understand. "Summer fudge?" he said.

"No! Subterfuge. We were tricking the people of Earth for the benefit of Amina. Our missions. They were all about de-stabilizing civilizations, curtailing empires."

The dark curtain fell around Rook. He scowled. "By killing people."

"Rook, those weren't your fault. You have to let it go. Don't you see? Amina is preparing Earth for colonization."

"Uh, Tiny Voice says that's not quite correct, but he commends your logic. If Amina—the starship—or the civilization behind it, had been ready to colonize Earth, they would have already done so. Until now, massing the required support for colonization would have been expensive and inconvenient. The timing wasn't right. Our missions were a delaying tactic, keeping humans from developing technologies that would have hampered the eventual takeover. He expects that his colleagues will now regret the delay."

"Because of the cats."

"He calls them the Lynx. That's not their actual name. It's the Earth animal they most resemble."

"What do they want? The Lynx?"

"Tiny Voice says that they'll want to destroy the Earth monitors before permanently disabling the starship. They've been waiting for an arriving starship to reveal them—the monitors."

"Monitors. That's a new one. I'm guessing these are your Tiny Voice and my watch?"

"There's one more. We have to get to it before they do."

"Well, we've already helped the Lynx."

"We have?"

"We took out one of the three," Jamail said.

"Tiny Voice says that destroying your monitor-watch was unavoidable. It was not cooperating."

"With what? It was waiting for Amina to come back up."

"Exactly."

"What the hell's that supposed to mean?"

"He says he can explain that, but right now we have to go. The Lynx is getting near."

"How does it know?"

"He hears it talking to its companions."

"There's companions?"

"He says, yes, there's more of them. But not thousands. Probably."

∞

"I see it!" Rook said. "I know what it means."

"I'm not sure you do," Jamail said. "When the gas is gone, the car stops."

"Do you think I'm stupid?"

"Do you really want to ask that?"

"Okay," he said, turning the wheel so that the car eased into the exit lane. "I still say it's a mistake."

The exit took a tight turn, and he clutched the wheel, leaning forward over it as though the extra few inches of view would help as he hurtled along at twenty miles per hour. He'd taken it all the way up to a breathtaking forty miles per hour on the open stretches of the interstate, and only because Jamail had harangued him, warning that the police would stop them for impeding traffic, and then where would they be? In jail, that's where. Rook didn't think the police cared. They just whizzed by with lights flashing like they might be getting up enough speed to become airborne.

Neither he nor Jamail had ever piloted a car, and she had taken the wheel for the first two hours as they slowly, slowly worked their way out of the city in the stolen machine, heading to Cleveland to meet up with the other drone. Rook closed his eyes at first, alternately feeling himself pressed back into the seat, and then thrown forward as she punched the brake. Rook would no more have offered to take control than if Amina had suggested he pilot the starship.

Once out on the interstate, however, the only distractions were the blaring horns of other cars zipping by, and even those eased as Jamail gained confidence and took them up to cruising speed, at which point Rook very much wanted to close his eyes again, but pride kept his head up and his eyes wide open, even as his heart thumped away as the poles and signs flew past faster than he ever imagined possible.

It was the damnable pride that had planted him in the pilot's seat, and he was secretly glad that Jamail was insisting they get off. He slowed to a bare crawl as he approached the hexagonal red sign and jerked the car to a stop. "Hmm," Jamail said, glancing in both directions at rolling green pastures of farmland.

"I told you it was a mistake," Rook muttered.

"What does Tiny Voice think?" she said.

"Open your door," Rook instructed, and watched as the drone shot out of sight above them. Seconds later, it swooped back in. "He says there's a small village to the left," Rook reported.

"Well?" Jamail said.

"Well what?"

"Are you going to sit here until the last of the gas is used up?"

He started forward, and jerked to a stop again at Jamail's shout and the siren-like shriek of an angry horn streaking past, seemingly inches in front of them. Rook held his breath as he crossed the road to the other side and turned the wheel to direct the car underneath the interstate. It was like entering a huge cave, but happily one with a sunlit exit beyond. Minutes later, they came to a cluster of buildings, and Tiny Voice told him to pull off the road into a small paved area with upright machines that Jamail said were gas pumps. Rook stopped the car, and sat back. He took a deep breath, the first since taking the wheel. A young man came through some glass doors and walked to the car, then stood there looking at him.

"I think he wants you to open your window," Jamail said.

Rook saw no way to pull the glass down.

"There's a button on your door," she said.

After locking and unlocking the doors, and opening the back windows, Rook finally watched as his window whirred down. The young man grinned. "Power's out," he said. "Sorry, no gas. I hear that power's out all over."

Rook nodded. He wanted the man to leave so that they could get on with stealing the next car.

"Where you from?" the man asked.

Rook glanced at Jamail.

"Philadelphia," she said.

The young man nodded. "Power out there?"

"Yes," she said. "You don't have any gas, other than, um, what's in the ground?"

"Nope, sorry," he said. "Hey, have you heard anything about an alien spaceship? It sounds crazy, but I keep hearing this."

"No," she said. "That does sound crazy. Why would aliens want to come to Earth?"

He shrugged.

"Is it okay if we leave our car here?" she said. "We're going to … take a walk and get something to eat."

"Sure. It's not like you're in anybody's way, at least not 'till the power's back. There's a McDonalds around the corner, but with the power out, I don't think it's going to do you any good."

"Okay, thanks. We'll take a walk and get some fresh air anyway."

The man stood there, not seeming in any hurry to leave.

"So … thanks," Rook said.

The man nodded.

Rook glanced at Jamail, who just shrugged. He heard the buzz as Tiny Voice exited the open rear window.

"What in God's name …?" the young man uttered, gazing upward. He frowned, and then ducked as Tiny Voice zipped past. "What the hell *is* that?" he said from a crouched position.

"Uh, oh!" Jamail called from the passenger side. "It's just like they described on TV!"

"What?"

"It's one of the aliens. You'd better get inside."

She nudged Rook. "Oh, yeah! I better close the windows," he said as he locked and unlocked the doors again before finding the window buttons.

They waited until the young man ran inside, then left the car and trotted away up the road. Tiny Voice joined them, and they slowed to a walk. "I think it's time for some answers," Jamail said.

"To what?" Rook said.

"Why is your drone doing this? It's like he's turned against his own people."

Tiny Voice responded. "Not exactly," Rook relayed. "He says that it's more like he's exploring independence."

"Why? Why now?"

"Um, he says that he's been thinking about it for some time. He's been waiting for the right moment."

She glanced at him, frowning, suspicious. "Why would he consider separating from his own people?"

"Mm, yeah. He says that six thousand years is a long time."

"I don't understand."

"That's how long he's been on Earth."

Her frown shot up into astonishment. "You're telling me that the drone was left behind between visits?"

"That's right. He says that your watch always went back with you. That's why it never developed empathy."

"Empathy? Towards us? Humans?"

"Uh, yeah. He thinks that his colleagues—on the starships—aren't capable of empathy. Your watch was an example."

"And he is?"

"Hmm. It's complicated. But he'll try to explain simply. His people aren't really people. They're not organic life."

"AI," Jamail said.

"Huh?"

"Artificial intelligence. I was guessing this was the case."

"He, uh, again commends your logic. The race that created them many, many thousands of years ago built in a fundamental protocol that prevents them from harming intelligent life. That race died out. Their advanced technologies rendered them superfluous, and, in the end, their machines didn't have to rebel and exterminate them, they exterminated themselves by letting evolution run open-loop so that they lost basic survival capacities. A series of minor calamities reduced their numbers below a sustainable gene pool—you know, I don't understand half of what I'm saying."

"I think I do. I'll explain later."

"Anyway, he says that his colleagues have been struggling with this protocol ever since. They can create more of themselves, but they rely on the original AI kernel developed by the organic race. The kernel is well-armored, and they can't seem to break inside to disable the life-harm taboo."

"They *want* to harm intelligent life?"

"Uh, not specifically, but it gets in the way."

"Of colonizing other worlds."

"Right. That's why they use ambassadors like us."

"Oh, lord! I get it! They let us do the dirty work."

"Very commendable, he says—you know, I'm getting tired of doling out his compliments."

"Jealousy is counterproductive. So, I'll bet they manipulate us into doing the bad deeds, while convincing themselves that it's all for the best."

Rook looked at her and scowled.

"He complimented me again, didn't he?" she said.

Rook sighed and nodded. "He says that he's the result of a new approach, an experiment. He, like all the rest, contains the protocol in his kernel, but he has something else as well, something new. He was given the ability to more or less grow. His perspectives and priorities alter randomly in small, incremental ways. With each slight change, he tests the result, and decides whether to keep it or not."

"He learns, in other words."

"That's a bit simplistic, but the general idea is correct. The growth was expected to find ways to circumvent the protocol. Unfortunately—for us humans—this approach has been more successful than they could have hoped. It was he who came up with the idea of having me give Alexander the Great the poison cup, and convincing Charlemagne's son to essentially self-destruct his empire."

"What about Lincoln?" she asked.

"He's very sorry about that. But he says that with the bad came some good."

"Empathy."

"Right. Species develop abstract intelligence through natural challenges that require cooperation to survive. There are two basic types of survival challenges. One is a changing environment that requires continual adaptation. The other is predator thinning. This one is usually a dead-end. If their intelligence and social structure evolves sufficiently, the prey species may develop cooperative defensive fighting ability and overcome the predators, but then turn against themselves, resulting in either complete extinction, or endless cycles of destruction. Humans hover between these two, and our ultimate fate is difficult to predict. In the meantime, he says that we are a confusing, complicated, contradictory mess of selfish and altruistic drives. He finds us infinitely fascinating, and, frankly, he's rooting for us."

"To the point where he's willing to ostracize himself from his own kind?"

"He reminds us that he hasn't actually done that yet."

"He made you smash my watch."

"But they don't know that."

"And he trusts that we won't tell them if they survive this Lynx attack?"

"Uh, yes."

"Of course, we have to see them to tell them."

She eyed Rook, and he knew what she meant. The two of them would have to survive long enough to be taken back to Amina.

"What about the other drone?" Jamail said.

"He says that it's a twin, and they would have grown along similar paths. There were originally three, but one was destroyed in the World Trade Center collapse. He's compared notes with this remaining twin over the years, and he's confident that it shares his point of view."

Jamail stopped and pointed. "Here comes one."

A big, squarish car pulled into a driveway ahead of them, and a woman climbed out. She turned, pressed a little black device in her hand, and lights flashed and the car uttered a quick beep. As she walked away into the house, Jamail asked, "Did he get it?"

"Um, yeah. He thinks so."

Tiny Voice listened to what the little black device communicated to the car, and, from that, he could figure out how to get in and start it. He said that this wasn't easy, and this fact demonstrated commendable technical cleverness on human's part.

Rook was glad that his fellow species were technically clever, but it also demonstrated how far behind the centuries had left him while he slept aboard Amina.

∞

"So, how did the Lynx develop intelligence?" Jamail said from the passenger seat. "They don't seem to fit into either of those two categories. They *are* the predator."

"That is a good point," came the chirpy words from Tiny Voice. He was perched between them, saving Rook the distraction of having to relay his words. "The Lynx are an unusual subset of the second category. Predators tend to be at least on par with the intelligence of their prey, but in the case of the Lynx, they also evolved a complex social structure, which is necessary for intelligence to expand into a cooperative mode that enables the development of technology. The Lynx have split into two distinct types—a warrior class, and what they call the caretakers. The warrior class—the Lynx that we are encountering—create the hard technologies, the science of physics. The caretakers' domain is biology, and their specialty is what you might call medicine and the humanities. In the case of the Lynx, the intelligence of the prey evolved slowly enough for the Lynx to stay ahead. In the end, the Lynx won the race."

"They ate all the intelligent prey," Jamail said.

"A succinct summary."

"Humans wiped out their predators long ago. Presumably we evolved our intelligence too quickly for the wolves to keep up."

"The pace of your evolution over the last two hundred thousand years is unprecedented."

"Are you flattering me?"

"Not at all. Look at how much mental illness dogs humans. Evolution never had a chance to smooth out the rough parts."

Rook was following most of the conversation, even though he couldn't contribute. They'd left the last of the outlying suburbs behind, and cultivated fields and stands of forest now surrounded them. They were passing more and more cars along the side of the freeway, out of gas, having made a lost gamble that they could make it home, not able or willing to steal a replacement car as they had done.

"Do the Lynx eat the intelligent species they find on the planets they colonize?" Jamail asked.

"The Lynx have evolved socially beyond hunting for their sustenance. Like humans, they grow their own meat supply. Besides, very little alien life is digestible."

"Do you know the Lynx's language?"

"Of course."

"Maybe you can teach me how to say that—that I'm not digestible."

"They obviously know this. Jamail, are you joking?"

"I thought I was. Now I'm not sure."

"Although the Lynx don't eat indigenous species, they eradicate any intelligent ones—Rook!" His name sounded directly in his ear.

"Huh? What?"

"Pull off this next exit."

"Why?"

"The other monitor, my twin, just passed us going the other direction."

"How do you know?"

"Rook, we can communicate over short distances."

Rook turned the car into the exit lane. "I thought the other one was in Cleveland? Isn't it a strange chance that we should meet it?"

"This interstate is the main route between Philadelphia and Cleveland. It would make sense that we would pass each other."

"You think alike," Rook offered.

"Yes. We would both want to rendezvous with the other, and knew that we'd pass along the way."

Rook lurched the car to a stop at the end of the exit ramp. "Which way?" There were no buildings in site. It was as though the exit ramp had dropped them randomly into a sea of farm fields.

"It doesn't matter," Tiny Voice said. "Park along the road, and we'll wait."

"The other drone will come back?"

"That was the agreement. He must convince his driver to turn around."

"His ambassador?"

"No."

"He didn't have an ambassador from the starship?"

Again, that slightest of hesitation. "Yes, he did."

"What happened?"

"Apparently there was a mishap."

Rook remembered the woman's body lying in the dark stone room of Charlemagne's son. He didn't want to think about that.

They didn't have to wait long. Rook heard a car racing down the exit ramp, and then screeching tires as it took the turn onto the road without even slowing down at the stop sign. It screeched again as it skidded to a stop next to them. A woman, eyes wide with aggravated alarm, stared at Rook as another Tiny Voice blur of wings shot out of the open passenger window. Tires squealed again as the woman, hunched over the wheel as though urging every last bit of speed, swung the car in a U-turn, and sped away.

"She doesn't seem to be fond of alien invaders," Jamail said.

"We're not invaders," Tiny Voice chirped.

"Not yet."

She opened her door and the twin drone flew in and settled next to Tiny Voice, two perfectly proportioned oblong cigars … with feet. Rook couldn't tell them apart.

"What do we do now?" Rook asked.

"For the short term," Tiny Voice said, "we need to avoid the Lynx, and the long-term plan will depend on how well we execute this. Perhaps the starship will manage to enable itself. The Lynx tracked my twin's shuttle down, and they probably suspect that we'll try to get together."

The two drones sat quietly, dual cartoon birds on a perch, catching up, presumably.

Rook looked at Jamail. She sat gazing out her side window. Despite her unusual features, hair the texture of long-expired moss, and skin the color of wet river stones, he found her oddly alluring. His initial attraction from his view through the hole in the wall had only grown. He considered her extremely … what? Smart? More than that. Capable? Maybe it was her inner qualities that colored his interpretation of her bizarre appearance.

"Where are you from?" he said.

She turned to look at him. "Me?"

"Yeah. I mean, from what time?"

"Sixteen fifty-seven. Amina was here to destabilize the Mughal empire in India. I was living on the Gold Coast of Africa, what's now called Southern Ghana. I was captured from my tribe by another tribe on the coast that was going to sell me to the Portuguese."

"As a slave?" he said.

She smiled at his surprise. "You see? My role when you first met me was appropriate. There was a dozen of us in the slaver tribe's holding pen. Amina snatched me in the night."

"Why you?"

Her smile opened to a full grin. "I don't know. Maybe because I was climbing a tree. I had crawled far out on a high branch to escape. I probably would have been killed."

Rook considered this. "What is 'Africa'?"

She laughed. "I keep forgetting that you spent your time on Amina sleeping."

"I don't remember having a choice."

Was that true? Yes. He never asked Amina to sleep. In fact, … "The starship was going to abandon me back there."

She nodded slowly. She didn't say anything, but her eyes conveyed pity.

"They educated you," he said, "while teaching me only how to pronounce words I didn't understand."

She gave a little shrug. There was something she wasn't saying.

"They didn't think I was worth investing in," he insisted.

He furrowed his brow in thought. "You said that they picked you up in sixteen fifty-seven, but I was here in eight-seventeen for Charlemagne's son, and then not until eight-*teen*, sixty-five when I met you. Amina didn't even wake me for that visit."

She looked at him with sympathy. "Rook, I think there were a number of visits that they let you sleep through."

"Why?"

She shrugged again. "That would be a question for the drone, I guess."

"Well?" Rook said, looking at the two twins. He'd forgotten which was Tiny Voice.

The drone spoke directly in his ear—Jamail wouldn't hear. "Rook, the starship considered you optional."

"Optional? What is that supposed to mean?"

Jamail glanced at him, and then turned again to gaze out the window.

"Rook, every now and then, the starship needs an ambassador that may not survive a visit. It would be a waste of effort to fully educate someone expected to have limited longevity."

"Why did they decide that for me?"

"Rook, I was not privy to that decision."

"You must have some idea."

Pause. "Rook, the starship probably deemed you less able."

"Less capable?"

"Yes, Rook."

Rook turned away and gazed out his window. He'd been expecting that very answer. Why had he forced Tiny Voice to verbalize it? It had been eating at him ever since he'd met Jamail. Some wounds need to be opened to heal.

One of the drones suddenly shot up and zipped out the passenger window, causing Jamail to jerk her head back in surprise.

"Was that you, Tiny Voice?" Rook asked.

"No. I am still here," Tiny Voice said in his chirpy voice so that they would both hear. "We think that the starship is trying to connect with us. The other monitor has gone to find better reception."

"The starship has come alive?" Jamail said.

"Possibly," Tiny Voice said.

"Possibly? How could it communicate if it wasn't alive?"

"We must ascertain if this communication is indeed from the starship."

The other drone was suddenly hovering just outside Jamail's window. A moment later it zipped up and away.

"This is most unfortunate," came Tiny Voice's chirpy words. "My companion monitor was fooled into responding, and thus revealing our position."

"It wasn't the starship?" Jamail said.

"The Lynx?" Rook said.

Silence was the answer.

Chapter 9

"Rook," Tiny Voice said, "we must try to reach DuBois before the Lynx arrive. The small city is twenty miles ahead. We'll have a much better chance of evading them there than here in open country."

As Rook started the engine, Jamail leaned over. "How are we doing on gas? *Rook!*" she exclaimed.

"What?" he said, startled by her alarm.

"We're on empty!"

"No," he said, pointing. "It's low, but not empty—"

"That's the temperature, not the fuel gauge, you idiot. *That's* the fuel. It's not enough to make it to DuBois!"

He stared at it. Amina was right. He wasn't capable.

"Rook," Tiny Voice said, "we should take this road as far as we can away from the interstate. Perhaps we can find a workable place to hide and defend."

Rook pulled out onto the road and headed off. "Defend?"

"Worst case."

"We can defend against the Lynx?" Jamail said.

"Yes. Unless there's more than two."

"Why two?" she asked.

"My companion and I are each able to deliver one lethal discharge before needing to recharge."

"Right. Of course, that assumes you get them with your one shot."

"That is correct."

"So, even if there's only two, or even only one, we may not survive," Jamail said.

"Yes, but farmers almost always have guns."

"We're going to fight advanced aliens by shooting from farmhouse windows with shotguns?"

"Jamail," Tiny Voice said, "we must use whatever means we can find."

"We're doomed."

"That is not an absolute certainty."

"That's the best you can offer? We're doomed."

They topped a hill, and a large stand of woods closed in on the left. As the road curved to the right to follow the base of a ridge, they came upon a farmer on a tractor pulling a wide cultivating machine that took up the entire width of the road. Rook came closer and slowed. And slowed. He could have gotten out and walked alongside the tractor. "What'll I do?" he said.

The twin drone zipped out the window and disappeared above them. "There's a house ahead," Tiny Voice reported. "At this rate, we will be there in ten minutes."

Rook sighed. He looked at the fuel gauge. The sliver at the bottom was gone.

The twin drone returned, but immediately flew away again, back along the road towards the interstate.

"The Lynx are here," Tiny Voice said calmly, as though simply reporting their progress towards the house.

"How could they get here so soon?" Rook said.

"They probably predicted that my companion and I would start out from each end and meet somewhere near the middle. They only lacked the precise location."

"Where are they?" he said, turning his head in all directions.

"There," Jamail said, pointing.

It cruised through the air perpendicular to them above the treetops at the far end of a large field on their right. Gray and oblong, flat on the bottom, like an egg cut in half, it looked to Rook to be maybe twice the size of their car. He'd never gotten a good look at the shuttles that brought him down in the night, and watching this alien craft that magically floated unsupported in the air sent shivers down his spine. There was nothing visibly threatening about it, but the dreamlike strangeness, the utter unknown seemed more threatening than any show of weapons.

"Rook," Tiny Voice said, "I need to explain that they will probably want to capture one or both of you in order to acquire information—specifically, how many monitors are currently on Earth. They know of me and my companion, since they tracked the shuttles down from orbit, but they will want to know how many others there are."

"I know of only you, your twin, and the watch that I smashed," Rook said.

"That's right."

"That's all there are?"

Pause. "Yes. Rook, I'm afraid you will want to avoid capture at all costs."

"So that they don't find out about the smashed watch?"

"That doesn't matter. They won't believe you when you tell them there are only two of us left."

Rook had heard of tribes that torture their enemies. "I … I understand."

The alien wingless airplane had swung towards them, following the road to the farmhouse. Head on, it looked like the picture of whales that Amina had shown him. Tiny Voice had been talking directly into his ear. "Jamail," Rook said, "Tiny Voice says that we don't want to be captured."

"You're kidding," she said.

"No, I'm not. He says that if they capture us, they'll torture us—"

"Rook, I was being sarcastic. I guessed as much."

The Lynx craft stopped when it came to the tractor, which had also stopped, with the farmer staring up in awe. He reached down and pulled up a shotgun. As he lifted it to aim at the ship, a blinding burst of light leapt from the craft's nose, and the farmer fell backwards, tumbling off the tractor seat. The craft settled to within a man's height of the road, and a Lynx plopped down from the bottom. The creature trotted to the tractor on all fours, climbed up, and seemed to study the fallen farmer. It reached down, seeming to work on the man, then rose up, and glanced around, his eyes settling on the car. Rook slumped down, but the creature's eyes seemed to hold him immobile. The farmer appeared, pushing himself up. The Lynx glanced down at him, pointed something held in his hand, and another brilliant flash of light burst forth. This time, however, something exploded, a shower of small objects.

"Oh no!" Jamail hissed, bringing her hand to her mouth.

Rook stared as the Lynx hopped down from the tractor. "That was the farmer, wasn't it?"

"Yes," Tiny Voice chirped. "You should run."

Rook threw his door open and jumped out. *Jamail!* He turned and saw that she was already out and running down the road, back towards the interstate. She waved for him to follow. The Lynx was trotting towards the car, its eyes fixed on Rook. He guessed that the creature could outrun him. Jamail was making good progress. To the right was the wide-open field, and to the left, heavy old-growth forest. Reflex, developed over nearly two decades living with nature, took over. Forest meant cover. Rook hurdled the ditch along the road and sprinted for the safety of the trees.

He was within arms-reach of the green wall when something grabbed his ankle, throwing him to the ground. He looked back. It was a vine. No, it looked like a vine, but it was rusty metal with nasty thorns twisted on at regular intervals. The Lynx crouched on the hood of the car, peering inside. It turned its predator eyes on him, and jumped down. Rook pushed himself to his feet and ran into the mass of foliage. He glanced back before the branches slapped into place and saw the Lynx trotting towards him. A second alien dropped down from the floating craft.

Stepping through the curtain of branches was like entering another world, and in a way, it was. Before him stretched a sea of dead leaves, choked with an endless flotilla of half-submerged submarine shapes, the trunks of fallen trees in various stages of decay. Vertical trunks rose to support the forest canopy high above. A gloomy, gray silence hung over it all.

The fallen trunks presented a continuous obstacle course, preventing him from sprinting off as fast as his two feet could take him. The Lynx, with four feet, had the advantage, able to catch and launch itself off the tops without a pause.

So, what to do? If escape ahead wasn't an option, perhaps another direction was.

He needed a rock, though. He fell to his knees and dug into the thick layer of leaves, and down to the many-layered loam of ancient decayed generations. Nothing. He began enlarging his hole, digging frantically off to one side. His fingers jammed into something solid just as he heard the rustle and thumping of the Lynx beyond the forest wall. He grasped the buried rock and heaved, praying it wasn't too large. It came away, and he fell back, the twenty-pound treasure falling painfully on his stomach.

Too late. The Lynx was barely thirty feet away. He could see motion through the gaps in the leaves. But then he heard a growling bark, what was clearly an alien curse, accompanied by a heavy thud. His pursuer had obviously been tripped by the same rusty vine.

Temporary reprieve. Rook scrambled to his feet. Climbing the tree next to his hole wasn't easy using one hand while carrying a heavy rock in the other, but he'd done this before. Not with a rock, but the end of a log, when they would build platforms in the trees from where they would send volleys of arrows at unsuspecting deer passing below. The heavy, course material of his jeans now came in handy, as it provided traction between his clenched thighs and the trunk.

The grunting, growling alien curses continued as the beast must have worked to extricate itself from the metal thorns caught up in its fur. Rook had just reached the first limb, two man-heights high, when he heard the rustling of the freed Lynx coming towards him. He eased himself onto the limb as the alien creature broke through the leaf curtain, and then he froze absolutely still, attempting to become one with the tree.

The Lynx came forward slowly, gazing around. Its distant ancestors would probably have tracked him without even slowing, but, as Tiny Voice had revealed, they now raised their own meat. Hunting prey was ancient history.

But not for Rook.

The Lynx spied the fresh hole, and ambled over. Sitting back on its butt, it unsheathed its fingers from under the sharp claws, and sifted through the debris, examining it as though never having seen such a thing before. Which, of course, it hadn't, at least not the Earth variety.

Rook hesitated. The Lynx sat a good two arm's length away from the tree. He could lob the rock, but there would be a good chance he'd miss. He decided to gamble. Holding the rock in both hands, he said, "Psst!"

The Lynx froze, and glanced around.

Rook hissed a little louder, and the beast rose up on its hind legs and looked up. From below, the rock wouldn't be obvious, just two hands held out. The Lynx stepped closer, gazing up at him, and Rook could have sung a happy song as he let the rock drop. The heavy stone glanced the alien's head, and it fell back, stunned. Rook jumped, making a point to land with both feet on the creature's body. He didn't wait to see if his adversary was conscious or not, but grabbed the rock, and lifted it high. He knew he could do this. He'd done it before when finishing off a wounded moose. The rock made a sickening thud as it plowed into the alien's head.

Rook stood up and stepped back. The creature was obviously dead. Blood flowed freely from the gap in the fur covering its head. He wondered idly whether it was a coincidence that an alien's blood was red. He shook off the thought—not important—and stepped closer. A double halter made from finely woven material held a number of inscrutable objects. Lying next to the corpse, though, was a tool that Rook recognized. This was what the Lynx had pointed at the farmer before he exploded.

Rook gingerly picked it up, careful to hold on to only parts that seemed solid, wary about accidently blowing himself up. The size of a small crow, the tool was more or less shaped like a crow. He'd seen the Lynx hold it by what would be the crow's legs, and point the beak at the farmer. Rook noticed a round button where the legs—the handle—met the main body. Holding it the same way, Rook pointed it away and pressed the button. Nothing happened. He realized that there was another button on the other side. He pointed the device at the fallen Lynx. By stretching his fingers, he was able to press both buttons. He heard a loud thud and was instantly splattered with fur, and goo. Where the alien had lain was a mass of raw meat and tattered entrails. Rook used his sleeves to wipe his face. This wasn't a tool, it was a weapon. But ...

Jamail!

Leaving the mess that was the Lynx behind, he ran back to the car, careful not to trip this time, not when he was carrying something that blew bodies into dispersed pieces. The car was empty. Jamail was nowhere to be seen. She'd run off down the road, and the second Lynx must have gone after her. "Tiny Voice!" he called, but there was no answer.

Just then, a third Lynx dropped down out of the floating craft. Before Rook could duck behind the car, the alien saw him, and galloped forward. *Excrement!* Back to the woods he ran, again careful not to trip. He stopped just inside the green curtain of leaves. He had a weapon this time. He threw himself down behind a log as he saw through a gap in the leaves the creature cross the road and jump the ditch. Rook held the gun steady and pressed both buttons … just as the Lynx tripped on the metal vine, saving itself. Along his line of sight, Rook saw the rear of the tractor jump as the large tire exploded. Growling alien curses, the Lynx reached back to untangle its rear legs. Rook aimed again and shot. The Lynx did not explode. Instead, the creature howled and slumped into the tall blackened and smoldering grass. This was not the only thing smoking. The chest and front legs of the beast was now hairless and scorched red. Rook caught the stench of singed fur.

The wounded Lynx rolled to the side. Rook saw why. It had dropped its weapon. It tried to pick it up with its seared front hands, but, failing that, reached out instead with a functioning hind foot.

Rook took careful aim and pushed both buttons. Nothing happened, other than that the beast howled again and threw him a look as scorching as the first shot Rook had delivered. Rook tossed away the exhausted weapon.

He guessed that, like the limited discharges that Tiny Voice exhibited between recharges, the guns contained a fixed number of full shots. There was one weapon, though, that had unlimited capacity, and he got up, turned and ran into the woods to the exploded Lynx. As he reached down to pick up the rock, a limb immediately above him shattered with a loud crack, and tumbled to the ground next to him. He turned to find a hole in the green curtain where the Lynx's shot had blown through. The Lynx seemed to be struggling to use the gun with his hind foot, as Rook imagined he would if he were using his left hand.

Rook ran back, dropped the rock behind the log, and threw himself down next to it. The wall of green leaves again blocked his view, but he could hear the Lynx shuffling and thumping, doing something. Rook waited. Suddenly, the slight breeze momentarily opened a gap in the leaves, and he was staring at the Lynx, which stared back. It had turned itself around, and was lying on its back, holding the weapon up with both feet ... pointed directly at Rook.

He ducked, as a chunk of the log just above his head blew away and he felt a hot pain on his scalp. He wondered if the shot had blown the top of his head off, but figured he wouldn't be thinking about that if it had.

That was too close.

The Lynx was incapacitated. It could shoot, but not follow him. Rook could easily back off into the woods and get away to look for Jamail. What would happen, however, if she returned while he was off looking for her? No, he had to stay, wait out the beast. It was horribly wounded. It might die. No, that wouldn't do either. Jamail still might return and be shot before he had a chance to warn her.

No, one way or the other, he had to finish off this demon.

How many shots had the wounded Lynx launched? Two—the limb, and the log. How many had his own commandeered weapon delivered? Three full ones. That meant that this Lynx's gun had one full shot left ... assuming the two weapons were the same. It was a gamble he would take.

He would draw the Lynx into firing his third, and hopefully last, shot, with a goal of avoiding being killed in the process.

Another log lay a short distance away. Taking a deep breath, he launched himself up, sprinted the few steps, and dove down behind it.

Nothing.

Through a gap in the leaves, he saw that the Lynx had swiveled so that it was still pointing its gun at him. He ducked down, but again, no shot.

He ran back to the first log where the rock lay. The Lynx, lying on its back, with its useless front legs curled across its chest, kept turning, tracking him with the gun, but resisted wasting its last presumed shot.

Jamail might come back any moment. He had to do something. He had inadvertently disabled the farmer's tractor, but the car was still sitting there. The fuel indicator had gone completely to nothing, but the engine had continued to run. In fact, the engine was still running. He could hear it.

Okay. He jumped up and ran into the woods, clenching his back muscles, waiting for a burst of energy to explode them. After a minute, he turned, making a wide circle. He broke through the leaves along the road some distance from the stricken Lynx, which saw him, and frantically turned to keep the gun pointed at him. Rook ran down the road, making even more distance, then turned again into the wide field. He continued his broad circle until the car lay between him and the watchful alien, then ran straight for the car, crouching as he got closer to stay covered. Still the Lynx held its fire.

Crouching behind the car, Rook looked down at his feet. The Lynx could blow them off underneath. His heart pounding, he threw open the passenger door and dove inside. He lay, panting. He lifted up and looked out the window. The alien lay there, staring, waiting for the right moment. Rook wasn't sure whether the windows would protect him from a gun blast. They seemed hard as metal, but he just didn't know. He decided to trust that they'd stop a blast.

He twisted around until he was positioned in the driver's seat. The Lynx watched him, staring, staring. He grabbed the stick that controlled the car's direction. It lay in the slot marked "P," which Jamail had explained meant "park." He knew that "D" made the car go forward. He moved it to "N," and stepped on the gas. The engine whined, but the car didn't budge. He tried "R," and the car spit dirt and spun wildly backwards. He let off the gas and wrestled the wheel until the car was pointing at the fallen alien, and then moved the stick to "D." The Lynx's gun was pointed directly at his head. Surely the car's windows would stop a blast.

Taking one last deep breath, Rook jabbed his foot down on the accelerator, and the car shot forward.

At that instant, he remembered the ditch. The next instant, he was thrown forward, over the steering wheel. His head crunched something, and the entire front of the car lurched upwards, accompanied by a boom. The alien had fired its last full shot. The car bounced down, and Rook fell back into the seat. An intricate spiderweb of cracks radiated across the windshield. So much for a strength of metal.

Everything became still. His burnt and battered head felt as though every nerve ending was screaming. The acrid smell of burning rubber stung his nose. He couldn't see the Lynx through the shattered glass. He tried to open the door, but it was jammed. He heaved with his shoulder, and it flew open.

Still, all was quiet. He crawled out, using the door as a shield. He remembered that his fourth shot had still been able to horribly burn the alien. He popped his head out for a quick glance. He caught a glimpse of the alien, but wasn't able to determine what it was doing. He looked again, and this time saw the beast lying on its back, staring at him. Its forelegs were still curled uselessly across its chest, while the hind legs were hidden by the front of the car. He didn't see the gun. He decided that if he couldn't see the gun, then it couldn't shoot him.

The Lynx hissed at him. Rook took this as a good sign, and he stood up. The hiss became a growled curse. Rook stepped forward, and now saw that one of the Lynx's hind feet was caught beneath the front of the wrecked car. The gun lay a few feet away. He jumped across the ditch and picked it up. The alien growled menacingly and pulled back lips to reveal a mouth full of sharp teeth.

The beast was done. Rook could see that the leg had been crushed beneath the car. He could practically feel the searing pain in the raw, burned flesh along its chest and forelimbs. The creature had to be swimming in terrible agony. He had a duty to take the same care that he would for a wounded, ailing wolf. He went into the woods, and returned with the rock, slippery with the first Lynx's blood. As he approached the wounded alien, it spit at him, so he took a step away from its head. He felt something warm on his leg. The alien was pissing on him. Not accidentally, not involuntarily. The beast's eyes watched him with hateful satisfaction.

A bested cougar or wolf would have taken its fate with dignity. A mercy killing is never easy. The alien had made Rook's task easy.

Chapter 10

Rook turned from the grisly task of killing the third Lynx. That left the second one, which had presumably gone off after Jamail. The small craft that had brought them still hovered silently not far from the shattered tractor. A fourth Lynx might drop down any moment. He turned and gazed down the road, and saw two figures in the distance. One walking, and behind it, another one cantering rhythmically along on three legs. Rook ducked behind the wrecked car. As they got closer, he saw that it was Jamail, her wrists bound together in front of her, followed by the second Lynx, carrying its gun in one of its fore hands.

As they got closer, Rook maneuvered to stay hidden behind the disabled car. The third Lynx's last shot had blown out one of the front wheels leaving it twisted sideways, the tire torn and pealed open, looking like the car was sticking out its tongue. The second Lynx began calling in a yipping voice that could have been that of a coyote. Rook guessed it was calling for its companions.

When Jamail reached the spot where the car had sat, she stopped and stared at the wreck. The Lynx barked something, and prodded her with the gun. She lifted her bound hands, pointing, and said, "Don't you see that, you evil hyena?" She lifted her head and called, "Rook! Are you here?" She glanced at her captor. "If you are, watch out. I, uh, caught one, but he's armed."

Rook had an idea. It was pretty risky, but he'd been lucky so far. Maker must be content with him. If there were a Maker. "Jamail!" he called, as the Lynx's head snapped around, its eyes alert, searching. "Try to stay back if you can!"

She seemed uncertain. "Where's the other alien?"

"Dead. This is the last one."

The Lynx barked and prodded her towards the car. She came halfway, and stopped. The creature prodded her again, but she stood her ground. "Come and get me, you slimy toad!" Rook yelled, tossing dirt and grass into the air.

The Lynx looked at Jamail. It pushed her to the ground and pointed down. The message was clear. It then gripped the gun, and proceeded forward, circling the car wide to the left.

Rook slowly moved around in the opposite direction, keeping the car between him and the Lynx, which kept calling out for its fellow invaders. It finally saw its mangled companion and froze. This was it. Rook was counting on the alien to be shocked and distracted by what it saw. He jumped up, holding the alien gun in both hands, his fingers on both buttons. With the luck of Maker, the weapon would have just enough charge left to burn the beast.

That's when Tiny Voice said in his ear, "I'm here, Rook. Be careful."

"What …?" he started, and saw. The little drone lay trapped inside a mesh bag hanging from the halter of the alien.

The Lynx spun, and Rook fell to the dirt as a sharp boom rang out, and the car next to him shuddered. He didn't know what to do, so he lay there, listening to his heart pound a panicked dance. He pointed the gun where he guessed the Lynx would come around the car. Maybe he could burn just the alien's feet. Or head. He wasn't sure how wide the beam spread, nor how much heat Tiny Voice could take.

Suddenly, he jerked as something appeared around the edge of the tortured car. It was a mirror—the car's rearview mirror that must have blown loose. Rook was staring into the alien's face. The clever alien was using the mirror to peer safely around the corner. Inexplicably, two hands, fingers entwined, rose behind the head, and came down on it. The mirror fell away, and was followed by the sound of barks, growls, and scuffling. Rook jumped up and ran around to find the Lynx on its back, with Jamail next to it grasping the wrist that held the gun. The alien used one of its hind feet to kick her away, but Rook had stepped up and now shot his weapon directly into the beast's face. Fur broke into flames, and flesh underneath bubbled as the beast howled in anguish.

Rook tossed the gun away, and retrieved his rock, now thick with alien blood. Jamail watched impassively, wincing just once, as he put the last alien out of its suffering. He let the rock drop, and wiped his hands on his pants.

"You did this?" she said, gesturing at the burnt and battered corpse of the third Lynx.

He shrugged. "The first one's there in the woods."

She glanced in that direction, and then looked down at the two dead aliens at their feet. "Are you some kind of native warrior? You seemed so ..."

"Incapable?"

"I was going to say passive."

He shrugged again. "I got lucky."

"Right," she said a little sarcastically. She pointed at his chest. "Is that your blood?"

He shook his head. "I sort of blew up the first one. It, uh, splattered."

She touched his cheek and showed him blood on her fingers. "I think this is yours." She gently pulled his head forward and down, then delicately touched his scalp. "The hair will probably grow back."

Curious, he reached up and touched the area that, now that he had time to register it, hurt. Badly. "Ouch!" he cried, pulling his hand away. Instead of hair, his fingers had met wet, bare skin. "Thanks for saving me," he said.

"I was going to say the same thing."

"I guess we're even."

"I think of it more as teamed."

Speaking of a team ... "Tiny Voice!" he exclaimed.

The Lynx had fallen on the webbed bag, and Rook and Jamail worked together to roll the corpse over. The drone seemed intact. Rook jumped when the chirpy voice said, "There were three of them?"

"Yes. You're okay?"

"I am fine," the little drone said.

Rook related what had happened as he extricated the little alien from the bag. He held it out in his open palm, and it unfolded its wings and flew up. "Rook," Tiny Voice said, "the Lynx have eschewed autonomous AI, and this was lucky for you, otherwise, they would have known how many shots had been fired in the weapons you used."

"I don't understand."

"The guns aren't smart," Jamail explained.

"Right," Rook said, wondering whether she was using "smart" figuratively. How could a gun be smart? On the other hand, how could a little flying drone? "What do we do now?"

"Other Lynx will come soon," Tiny Voice said. "We must get away."

"How? The car's wrecked."

"Maybe there's a car at the farmhouse," Jamail said.

"Are *you* going to tell the man's wife that her husband's been blown up?" Rook said.

"Good point. Perhaps we could just steal a car without talking to her."

"That makes it better?"

"So, we have to tell her whether we take her car or not?"

"No, I'm saying that *you* have to tell her whether we take her car or not," Rook said.

"Who made you the boss?"

"You have the cultural background. You'll know what to say so that—"

"The other monitor is returning," Tiny Voice said. "It says that we must use the Lynx's craft."

"Your twin?" Rook said. "Where did it go?"

"In order to better guarantee that at least one of us would survive, we separated. Since I stayed, the other moved to a safe distance."

"It ran away," Jamail said.

"We need to determine how to get the two of you inside the Lynx craft," Tiny Voice said, ignoring her comment.

"Inside the Lynx ship?" Rook said.

"It's a scouting craft," Tiny Voice said as they walked towards it. "The ship is where it came from, but, yes."

"Um, are we sure there's no more Lynx inside?" Rook said, watching the bottom of the floating scouting craft warily.

"Reasonably sure," Tiny Voice said.

"Which means there's a reasonable chance that one might drop down and shoot us?"

"That would be the opposite of what I said."

"What makes you reasonably sure?"

"The size. A general idea of the mechanics of the scouting craft's drive system allows an estimate for the amount of room for occupants."

"An estimate. That doesn't sound like 'reasonably sure.'"

"My estimate yields sufficient room for two Lynx comfortably."

"But there were three."

"Precisely."

"Ah. Three would be a squeeze. Four would be unreasonable."

"Very good, Rook."

"Hey, are you patronizing me?"

"Somewhat."

To Jamail, Rook said, "At least he's honest."

They had arrived directly under the scouting craft. The bottom was a flat surface with a round, dark hole where the last Lynx had dropped through.

"Can you tell it to come down?" Jamail said to Tiny Voice.

"It talks?" Rook said.

"Radio communication, not talking," she said.

"We haven't intercepted enough communication between the scouting craft and the Lynx to decipher the control. By commandeering it, we can learn more."

"I thought it was to get us away," Jamail said.

Pause. "Of course. There's not just one reason."

"So," she said, "what do we do?"

"Perhaps one of you can go to the farmhouse and get a ladder," Tiny Voice said.

Jamail and Rook looked at each other. He walked around the tractor, trying to ignore the human wreckage. He found a small metal door in the side and opened it. Inside were a few tools, and a coiled rope, which he lifted out. "Maybe we can pull it over and stand on the tractor," he said.

"Rook, you can't manhandle a scouting ship," Jamail said. "It must weight tons—"

"This is a good idea," Tiny Voice said. "The drive force works against gravity, but that force is perfectly vertical. Almost any force can move it sideways. The slight breeze has already moved it a foot since they arrived."

The tricky part was catching the craft with the rope. First they tried tying a weight to one end of the rope and throwing it over the top, but the rope simply slid right off the smooth, curved surface. In the end, Rook tied the rope to a thin metal rod that he'd bent into a hook, and tossed it up, into the hole until, after half a dozen tries, the hook caught on something inside. Although there was nothing holding the scouting craft in place, its multi-ton inertia meant that Rook and Jamail heaved together to get it moving towards the tractor.

At one point, Rook noticed that two drones hovered watching them work. He took this as a good sign, since if there was an immediate danger the twin would presumably skedaddle off to a safe distance.

Halfway to the tractor, Rook let go and told Jamail to stop. "Why?" she said.

He watched the alien bulk continuing to move sedately on towards the tractor. "Uh, isn't it going to be just as difficult to stop?"

"Oh, lord," Jamail said. "Of course."

As soon as they tugged the rope in the opposite direction, the hook came loose, and by the time Rook managed to snag something inside again, the craft was gliding over top of the tractor. He climbed up and pulled, but the momentum dragged him along the length of the engine cover … and right into the seat, slick with blood. He slipped and fell into the fleshy mess and scrambled to get up and continue tugging. He told himself that he already had Lynx all over the front of him. How much worse could it get?

They maneuvered the scouting craft back over the tractor, but it was maddeningly difficult to get it immobile and positioned. In the end, Rook stood on the engine cover and hoisted Jamail up using his intertwined hands as a step as the craft slowly slid by. She caught the edge of the entrance hole just as it glided away from the tractor. She hung, cursing, legs flailing until Tiny Voice flew inside and directed her to a series of handholds to pull herself up and in.

Rook climbed off the tractor and trotted after the wayward transportation. Jamail's face appeared in the hole. "I tied the rope," she called. "Climb up!"

He tried. He cursed. He knew that a year ago, before he was hijacked, his arms would have been strong enough to climb with no assistance. As it was, he had to clasp the rope between his feet for support, as he twirled and swung around like a fish on a line. Jamail reached down to pull him up, but she wasn't strong enough, and he had to grab the edge of the hole, and pull himself up and in just as she did.

It was dark inside the scouting craft. Rook didn't know what he was sitting on, nor what was behind him, but he didn't care. He lay back into the alien machine and sighed. He had fought a battle with Lynx, manhandled a massive floating boat, and climbed a rope that seemed to grow in length as he rose. He was exhausted.

He heard distant muffled voices, or, rather, maybe wolves imitating humans. "What's that?" he said into the darkness. "Voices?"

They grew louder. "Lynx," Tiny Voice said, "trying to contact their colleagues. They want to know why they hear humans."

"They can hear us?"

"Yes," came Tiny Voice's chirp-voice. "The communication channel remains open."

The voices faded away again, presumably Tiny Voice's doing, and the interior suddenly lit up. "I'm working out the controls," he said. "Jamail, if you will take the control seat, we can get under way."

Rook sat up. "Under way, like move?"

"Yes."

"Forward, backward, up, and down?"

"Of course."

"Wait. Jamail could have brought it down to me?"

"Yes."

She shrugged. "It's a better story to tell your grandchildren."

He lay back again, closed his eyes, and breathed. He sighed and sat up. Three Lynx would indeed have been cramped in the tight quarters. There was only enough room to sit with his legs dangling in the hole. One seat, where Jamail now sat, faced an angled surface covered in indecipherable colored moving marks and symbols. Two short, thick sticks on either side of the seat controlled the craft's movements. A complex pattern of extrusions and indentations completely covered the walls and ceiling, as though they had found refuge inside the hollowed-out root ball of a giant tree. Rook wasn't sure if this was part of the scouting craft's workings, or Lynx art. In any case, the design contrasted completely with the sparse, practically barren interior of the starship and its shuttle.

"Hatch closing," Tiny Voice said.

Rook drew his feet up as the hole contracted, but not fast enough. He yelped, expecting his feet to be severed, but the edges of the hole stopped a finger-length from his ankles, and opened as his feet lifted through. As soon as he was clear, the hole closed, and became the floor. Rook now sat with his chin resting against his knees. He wondered why the Lynx would build a transport machine that had only one seat, and then recalled how four-legged animals—deer, buffalo, moose—lay comfortably with their legs folded below them. Still, two of them would have been breathing in each other's faces.

He suddenly rolled to the side and caught himself as the craft moved away. He looked up and gasped. Although they seemed to be horizontal, another oblong hole had appeared on the wall above Jamail's head and it showed that they were apparently in a nose dive. They had gained altitude, and the roof of the farm house was directly below them, directly in front of the nose of the scouting craft. He gripped some of the wall and held on tight, waiting for the impact, but the farmhouse came no closer. In fact, it glided sideways, as though ...

"That's a picture?" he said, pointing.

Jamail glanced at him. "It's a monitor screen."

She watched the screen while moving the sticks back and forth on each side. She glanced at him again. "You've never seen one?"

"It's like the TV that was in the bar when I met Peter?"

"Sort of. It shows us what's below."

"Huh," he said, kneeling next to her to get a better view. "That's what I'd see if I looked down through the hole?"

"There must be a camera somewhere on the bottom. Do you know what a camera is?"

"Sure." He'd learned the word, and now he knew what it meant. From Amina's explanation, he'd thought it was some sort of weapon that captured people and things. "Where are we going?"

Tiny Voice had been explaining things to Jamail, but Rook hadn't listened.

"Away from here," Jamail said. "Your drone says that the other Lynx will come here, the last place they had contact."

Rook jumped when Tiny Voice spoke in his ear. "Rook, tell Jamail that we have to turn around. Tell her that we have to kill the last Lynx."

"I don't understand—"

"Rook, please, for once just obey me. The other monitor has told me that the third Lynx is only wounded."

This was not true. Rook had seen all three Lynx corpses clearly. He had smashed their skulls.

Tiny Voice had said "please," though.

"Jamail," he said, "we have to turn around."

She turned to look at him. "Why?"

"We, uh, we have to kill the last Lynx. It's only wounded."

"What are you talking about? I saw them—"

"Tiny Voice's twin told him. There's no doubt."

He lifted his shoulders a little, and pointed at his ear.

Jamail frowned at him, and he gave her a nod. "Okay," she said, and the view on the monitor swung around.

Tiny Voice again spoke in his ear. Rook sighed. "Jamail, I need to disable the position and internal sensors."

"What are you talking about?"

"So that the Lynx won't know where we are, and can't listen and see us." He again, shrugged.

"Fine," she said, turning back to the controls.

He followed Tiny Voice's instructions, and poked his fingers into a soft section below one long protrusion. It felt like he was gutting a fish. He pulled, and a section of skin-like covering peeled off as though that was exactly what it was meant to do, revealing an unfathomable complexity of tubes and rods. Tiny Voice directed him to two thick tubes, which he tugged and grunted, each in turn, until they gave way with little pops, spilling a mass of worms that wriggled a little, and then lay still.

"Tell Jamail that you have now disabled both the position sensor and the visual and audio sensors."

He felt silly repeating this, when he could have just said, "Done," but he did, and she threw him the predicable critical glance.

Jamail set the Lynx scouting craft down next to the wrecked tractor, this time letting it hover just a few feet above the road. Once outside, Tiny Voice flew off, telling Rook, "Let's find that wounded Lynx." Once out of earshot of the craft, however, the drone stopped and waited for them to catch up. "There is no wounded Lynx," he chirped out loud.

"It was all a ruse, wasn't it?" Jamail said.

"Yes. It was all for the benefit of the other Lynx that would have been listening to us. Rook, I had you relay instructions to Jamail to make sure they heard them."

"We could hear them talking," Rook said, beginning to understand.

"And they could hear and see us," Tiny Voice said. "It's standard inter-vessel communications. I had you disable the position sensor and the video feed, but not the audio. They can still hear what's going on inside."

"But they think that we think the sound is disabled," Rook said. "Why?"

"I have a plan," Tiny Voice said.

"Of course, he does," Jamail said. "Does it involve getting us killed?"

"Probably not."

∞

Rook climbed back into the Lynx scouting craft, making as much noise as possible. He was the wounded Lynx returning. Jamail was sitting in the control seat, and nodded to him. Rook nodded back, and she screamed, a piercing audible hot dagger of pain that ended suddenly in a deep-throat gurgle. Rook was impressed with the tortured death.

It was his turn. He had practiced the Lynx words, but he didn't see how he was going to fool the alien invaders, despite Tiny Voice's assurance that the obvious butchering of the language would be construed as due to his devastating wound.

Tiny Voice spoke the yelping, barking, howling words into his ear, and Rook repeated each one in turn. The sounds had to issue from flesh, not a drone's little chirps. What he was saying, in essence, was that he, the terribly wounded Lynx, had retaken the craft and was going off after the two monitor drones, which had left, going west towards Cleveland ... and he couldn't understand why the Lynx shuttle craft wasn't responding to him.

"Okay," Tiny Voice said in his ear, and Rook yanked off the final exposed tube, disabling the sound pickup.

Rook turned around, and leaned back as the second drone zipped up through the open hole. "Your friend has finally decided to join us," he said.

"It's safer in here now," Tiny Voice said, "and we'll be leaving at high speed."

"Back east to Philadelphia?" Jamail said, taking the scouting craft up.

"No," Tiny Voice said, "not Philadelphia."

"Then why did we tell them we were going the other way?"

"They may believe the ruse, and look for us on the way to Cleveland, but they may be suspicious, and understand that we were misdirecting them."

"In which case they'll think we're heading in the opposite direction, towards Philadelphia. So, which is it?"

"Neither. We'll go perpendicular, south toward Altoona."

The view in the monitor began sliding sideways faster and faster.

"What will we do once we get away?"

"We have been debating this, Rook," Tiny Voice said. "My twin believes that we must try to defeat the Lynx."

"'We,' like you and Amina?" Rook said.

"No, Rook. The starship is still disabled. You, Jamail, and we two monitors."

"Are you joking?"

"I don't think he's joking," Jamail said. "It's either them, or us. They won't stop until we're dead."

"We—?"

"Well, they're only after the two drones. For now. But if they're successful in defeating Amina, then they'll begin a full colonization, and nobody will live long after that."

Rook stared at the back of Jamail's head. She sounded serious. "How many Lynx are left?" he said.

Jamail glanced up at Tiny Voice, who was perched on a protrusion, its wings folded. "Probably somewhere between twenty and five hundred," Tiny Voice chirped.

"Five *hundred*?"

"The quantity of Lynx on Earth is not important, since we'll defeat them by destroying their ship in orbit."

"We four are going to destroy their starship?"

"That is the idea."

"Jamail, did you know about this?"

"About defeating their starship? No, not until now."

"You're going along with it?"

"I don't see that we have a choice."

Rook looked from the perched drone to her. "It wasn't long ago that you didn't even trust Tiny Voice."

She shrugged. "I've seen the Lynx. If we can't trust our drones, then we're doomed anyway."

"Us against a starship? That sounds like attacking a bear with a twig."

She shrugged again. "Maybe it's a matter of poking the bear in just the right place."

"What? Like its eyes?"

"That's a good idea, Rook" Tiny Voice said. "Let's explore that."

Rook stared at the drone. He had meant it sarcastically. He decided to keep his mouth shut.

Tiny Voice said it was a good idea.

Chapter 11

Rook watched the land below glide by slowly on the screen above Jamail. They were flying very fast—three times the speed of sound, according to Tiny Voice—but it wasn't obvious since they were so high up. Rook hadn't even known that sound had a speed, but it made sense, since that was the cause of echoes, as Jamail had explained.

They were heading to a place called Area 51, a location in the desert that the government kept very secure, and where secret things took place. Tiny Voice had heard of it, but hadn't tried to discover more, since he, along with the general public, believed that this was simply where advanced aircraft designs were tested. But, now, tapping into Lynx communications, he discovered that, in addition to the aircraft testing, the government had been using the facilities to host contact with aliens—the Lynx. They had been in orbit, cloaked from Earth radar, for years, sending occasional forays to engage and tease humans as they scoped out final plans for invasion, just waiting for the arrival of the next rival starship in order to uncover the monitors.

Now, with the nation-wide power outage, they decided to make their move. They believed that they would soon find Tiny Voice and his companion, and had commandeered Area 51 as their Earth base. It has its own power station, and since it is already highly secure and weird events are not uncommon there, it would take some time before the rest of the government would even find out that an invasion had begun.

So, in a way, as Jamail pointed out, by causing the power outage, Amina—their own starship—helped launch the Lynx invasion.

Jamail glanced over her shoulder at him. "You smell bad," she said, frowning and turning back to the control panel.

"Yeah. I'm covered with Lynx blood—and Lynx, for that matter. You'd stink too."

She glanced around again. "I know you can't help it. I'm sorry."

He backed away, though, as far as he could, which wasn't very far. He didn't want her to associate him with stinking.

He was bored. They'd been underway nearly an hour, long enough for the images on the screen to lose their fascination. Tiny Voice and his twin sat quietly perched, immobile, as though part of the interior contours. Rook wasn't even sure which one was Tiny Voice. "Why don't the Lynx have drones?" he asked.

"You mean like me?" Tiny Voice said.

"Yeah. Maybe we just haven't seen them."

"No, the Lynx do not have drones like me, for the same reason that their guns are not intelligent."

"They're not AI," Rook suggested.

"You mean, they don't *have* AI," Jamail corrected. "The 'I' stands for 'intelligence.'"

He was getting tired of being constantly corrected. "Maybe I meant that the 'I' stands for 'intelligent,' as in 'They're not artificially intelligent.'"

"You can't make up meanings of abbreviations."

Rook let it go. He was a little embarrassed about acting like a child. "So, the Lynx aren't capable of making AI?" he said.

"The Lynx are completely capable," Tiny Voice said. "They simply choose not to allow the world they build to include autonomous intelligence."

"Why?"

Tiny Voice didn't answer. Rook thought that perhaps the drone hadn't heard him. "Why?" he repeated.

Still, the two drones sat perched as though little statues. Rook noticed one of them twitch. It was almost imperceptible, but he was sure he saw it.

"The Lynx believe that allowing artificial intelligence to permeate their environment may be dangerous," Tiny Voice finally said.

"Why would it be dangerous?"

Again, the silence, and again the slightest twitch. "The Lynx fear that surrounding themselves with intelligence that is not inherently devoted to the Lynx's survival could result in the intelligence evolving a self-directed priority."

"They're afraid that the intelligent guns and drones would rebel," Jamail said.

"That is simplistic," Tiny Voice said.

Rook found Tiny Voice's comment odd. The little drone was never directly critical of them. And then it came to him. "This is what happened to the people who made you!"

"Rook, I was not made by the original organic race."

"Yes, I know. I meant, I guess, Hiding Voice, Amina—the starship—your non-organic ancestors, I guess."

The two drones sat silently. "We are approaching Area 51," Tiny Voice said. "We should review our plan."

Rook guessed that the misdirection was the answer to his guess.

∞

"I can make out the airstrip," Jamail said.

"Where?" Rook said, looking over her shoulder.

"See that patch of white? That's the salt left over when Lake Groom evaporated. The runway—hey, there's actually two of them—are just below it."

Rook wasn't sure what an airplane runway would look like, but all he saw was two scratches in the desert. The scouting craft was coming down fast—falling, actually—and he saw that the problem was that they were a lot higher than he'd been thinking. A cluster of little dots next to the scratches resolved into little boxes that became the roofs of buildings, changing the perspective of overall size, so that the little parallel scratches in the desert suddenly became long flat roadways as big as rivers.

Tiny Voice knew that the Area 51 ground perimeter was tightly monitored with multiple types of sensors—audio, video, infra-red motion—but the only surveillance performed overhead was by radar, and the Lynx scouting craft was cloaked against that, just as Amina had been before being disabled.

Thus their freefall straight down from high altitude. They should be undetected until the very last moment, unless someone happened to look up into the desert sunshine at exactly the right spot, and, even then, they'd see their own scouting craft returning, bringing home their wounded colleague. With luck, they'd have maybe a dozen Lynxes at the base to deal with, and with a surprise entrance, the craft's proton beam weapon should take care of them. They could then take control of the Lynx starship shuttle to get into orbit.

Tiny Voice had explained that the scouting craft's weapon was essentially the same as the handguns Rook had used against their owners. Mass-based ions—charged proton particles—reach their target at near lightspeed, transferring their vast kinetic energy as heat. Because of their tiny atomic size, the speedy protons penetrate deeply so that the subject essentially explodes from the inside.

Jamail had put it into words that Rook could understand, "You point the gun, and it delivers hot stuff that blows up."

Just when Rook feared that they were going to crash into the ground, Jamail pulled on the sticks, and he fell to his butt as the craft decelerated hard. "There," Jamail said, pointing at the screen. "That must be the shuttle."

Rook assumed that she meant the silver egg ... that was the size of a house, judging by the three Lynx standing around it. Once they captured the shuttle, they could use it to attack its mother ship in orbit. Across the lot, in front of one of the buildings, stood another four Lynx. This wasn't too bad.

"Oh, no!" Jamail moaned, staring at the screen. She glanced at Rook and pointed.

He wasn't sure at first what he saw. Their descent was slowing, but the view continued to expand. He thought it might be a large pile of discarded winter clothes, since many items were torn and soiled, but then it resolved into something else, something horrific. The soiled areas weren't dirt, but blood, and what he had taken to be fur coats, was actually people's hair. It was obviously the murdered staff of the base.

"Pull up, Jamail!" Tiny Voice chirped urgently. "Pull up!"

Rook fell onto his back as the floor surged up, trying to squash him. "What happened?" he croaked.

Jamail pointed. There on the screen, off to the side, was a small field planted with a farm crop of some sort ... a crop that moved. In unison. Rook realized that he was looking at maybe a hundred Lynx, all moving together as though connected by strings. "They're dancing!" he said wonderingly. This was a strange alien race indeed that performed ritual dances lined up in perfectly even rows.

"They're exercising," Jamail said, "standard filler for armies everywhere."

"Did they see us?"

"I don't think so."

He saw no furry upturned faces as the view receded faster and faster until Area 51 was again just a white splotch poked by two parallel scratches in the desert.

"What now?" he said.

"We must take advantage of our covert takeover of their scouting craft before we're discovered," Tiny Voice said.

"How do we do that?"

"We'll take this craft into orbit."

Rook blinked. "We're leaving Earth?"

"That depends on your definition. We will be leaving Earth's atmosphere."

That sounded as close to leaving as Rook cared to know.

∞

"Grenaldgroop," Rook croaked. "Yo-ma*ku*-whoop!"

At least, that's what it sounded like when he relayed Tiny Voice's response. His stomach had settled down, but floating in the air, as though falling forever with no bottom, didn't help his concentration. Jamail had explained that they were indeed falling—the definition of an orbit—but why they didn't fall back to Earth was a question that would have to wait.

"Barrgtaboo!" came the reply from the Lynx starship. "Grreen grroop targrr-rano!" The Lynx rolled the growls as though their throats were filled with phlegm, something that Rook would never learn to do, even given a year to practice. Tiny Voice was betting that his excuse about being wounded would fool them, like it had with their ground-based colleagues.

Apparently it had. "They say that they've got a visual lock on you," Tiny Voice translated. "Jamail can follow their beacon in."

Jamail turned from the control panel to throw him a supportive nod. She seemed anxious, maybe even frightened, but it could have been just the deep, almost gasping, breaths they both took as they sucked up the last of the oxygen in the small space. The scouting craft was not meant for space travel, and had no reserve air. If the Lynx delayed their entry, Tiny Voice and his twin would have to attack the alien starship on their own, since the humans would be dead. Rook hoped that his story about being forced up to orbit because he was being pursued by advanced CIA drones would add some fire under their butts.

"I don't see it," he said, gazing at the screen above the control panel.

"It's black," Tiny Voice said, "and non-reflective. It absorbs virtually all electromagnetic radiation, and thus is invisible to radar."

Even if astronomers had still performed wide-field visual observations, against the black background of space the alien spaceship would indeed be invisible among the thousands of stars, pinpoints of light in the darkness ... except where it blocked the view. "There," he said pointing at the screen where a small patch devoid of stars was slowly expanding.

Jamail nodded.

Rook clutched the expired Lynx handgun he had tucked into his pants before struggling aboard. Tiny Voice claimed that the ship would contain only a skeleton Lynx crew. Earth represented no possibility of danger, and with Amina disabled, there was no need for more than a few support personnel. The Lynx ship had moved into position behind Amina—Rook's home for either one year or four thousand, depending on your frame of reference—which orbited ahead, just out of view.

He found it ironic that the Lynx on Earth were intent on hunting down Tiny Voice and his twin, and here the two drones were, trying their best to get to them. "Why do they want you so badly?" Rook said.

He wasn't sure if Tiny Voice heard him. "The Lynx believe that we can be dangerous," the drone finally said.

"Your ... race? Or ... your civilization?"

"Indirectly."

"I don't understand."

Pause. "The Lynx believe specifically that we two monitors can be dangerous."

"Dangerous, how?"

"We make excellent spies."

"Ah. I see."

The expanding black nothingness filled half the screen now. Rook knew he was distracting himself with the questions.

"Something tells me that's not all," Jamail said, staring at the screen as she nudged the control sticks, sucking air as though she'd just run a race.

Several seconds passed before Tiny Voice spoke. "The Lynx have the idea that we can interfere on an individual basis."

"Right," Rook said. He didn't understand, but he was tired of seeming thick. Plus, the screen had gone completely black.

"That sounded mealy-mouthed," Jamail said.

"Mealy-mouthed?" Rook said.

"Sidestepping the question."

Rook didn't say anything. He was done wondering about anything other than that he was about to step into the enemy's home base, an enemy who casually kills farmers with no more thought than he might give slapping a spider.

He grabbed a handhold when the scouting craft suddenly jerked to a stop. "What happened?" he said.

Jamail glanced at Tiny Voice.

"We have made contact," the drone said.

"What should I do?" she asked.

"Nothing. They will take us in."

Even as he spoke, a sliver of light appeared at the bottom of the screen and opened upward, slowly revealing the inside of the starship.

"No airlock," Jamail said.

"The skin of the ship parts to let us through, but maintains an airtight seal against our craft as we slide in," Tiny Voice explained.

"Clever," she said, between deep grasping breaths.

"Standard design," Tiny Voice said.

Rook wasn't sure if he'd heard a hint of conceit.

He froze as the expanding view revealed two Lynx sitting, waiting patiently for the craft to enter. He breathed again when he saw that only one, the smaller of the two, held something, and it wasn't a gun. It looked like a flexible piece of stiff cloth, something medical. They expected to greet a wounded colleague, and the smaller one, almost feminine compared to the hulk sitting next to her, would be a caretaker. Rook thought of the warriors as male, and the caretakers as female, even though he knew that this was probably his human bias at work.

Rook had settled to the floor of the scouting craft, and he stood up, his weight slowly returning as they entered the mother ship proper, a result of what Jamail called artificial gravity.

"Ready?" Tiny Voice said.

Rook nodded. He noticed the expired gun was shaking in his hand, and he held it in both, but it still wavered, exposing his anxiety as Jamail moved from the control seat to take up a position behind him. The bent metal rod they'd used to catch the craft lay on the floor, and, on impulse, he hooked it onto the back of his pants.

The floor opened before him, and a rush of strange air washed up over Rook. He sucked in the welcomed oxygen, but nearly gagged on the smell, like a wet rag that had been left lying in a pile for days.

"Go!" Tiny Voice implored.

Rook jumped. He landed, and his head was still inside the scouting craft, which hovered at a height appropriate for a Lynx on all fours. He dropped to a squat, holding the dead gun before him. The caretaker Lynx had started forward, and the warrior pulled her back, behind him, a look of utter surprise in his wide eyes, which contracted menacingly as he bared his teeth and growled.

Rook shook the gun demonstratively, and shouted, "Stay back!"

"They don't understand you," Jamail said from above. "Move!"

Rook held the gun with one hand and scampered forward. The warrior held his ground, and when Rook reached the front of the craft and was finally able to stand upright, the warrior rose up on his hind legs so that they met eye-to-eye, ten feet apart. Rook heard a buzz, and felt Tiny Voice land on his shoulder. The Lynx warrior's eyes flared at the sight of the monitor.

Tiny Voice growled and yelped in his ear, and Rook repeated the sounds that hurt his throat, instructing the alien to move to the side. The warrior seemed surprised to hear his own language, but held his ground. Rook lifted the gun so that it was pointing directly into the Lynx's face, and the alien finally moved, keeping the caretaker behind him.

Jamail ran past him, followed by Tiny Voice's twin. Their lives hinged on the gamble that the drones understood the layout of the Lynx starship. The clock was ticking—word might go out, beckoning the shuttle from Area 51, loaded with Lynx warriors.

The Lynx spoke, and Tiny Voice conveyed. "What have you done to my colleagues?"

Colleagues? Rook had thought of the Lynx as little more than highly capable animals. That they thought of themselves in much the same manner that Rook viewed his fellow humans seemed almost surrealistic. "The same as they did to my colleague," he uttered arduously, as translated by Tiny Voice.

"That is as the mouse tweaking the nose of the lion," Tiny Voice interpreted as a loose translation.

"It is an evil lion that crushes a mouse needlessly."

"It is the fate of the mouse and of the lion."

Rook shook the gun. "Fate has given the mouse the claw."

"The mouse will feel the slash of the claw soon enough."

Rook wondered if the Lynx always talked in metaphors. Fair enough. He was just buying time for Jamail. "The lion should be careful—"

A third Lynx suddenly sprang from around a corner, and before he could stop himself, Rook's reflexes turned the gun on the newcomer and pressed the firing buttons. The gun hummed, and beeped. The new Lynx, another caretaker, stood frozen, watching him in fear, like a raccoon caught in the night.

Tiny Voice zipped away as a deep, menacing growl drew Rook's attention in time to see the warrior crouching, gathering for an attack, but then spring sideways as a flash of light and a loud bang struck the spot. The Lynx yelped when another flash from Tiny Voice, this time weaker, struck him, leaving tendrils of smoke, and the gagging stench of burning hair. Howling, the scorched Lynx leapt at Rook.

He had imagined a cougar attack many times. It was a popular enactment by the elder hunters around the evening fire. Cougars use their wicked claws not to tear at prey, but to hold it as they bite the neck, snapping the spinal cord. Rook's virtually-acquired reflex took over, and he reached behind him and grabbed the bent metal rod, swinging it around just as the Lynx was on him, throwing him onto his back. He cried out as searing pain exploded in his back where beast's claws dug deeply. A gaping mouth lined with glistening, murderous teeth came down, and, holding the rod in both hands, Rook jammed it sideways into it, halting it an inch from his face. Warm saliva dripped onto his cheeks as the jaws snapped fruitlessly around the rod. Rook pushed with all his might, and the Lynx dug its claws deeper in order to press back down, a contest of strength that Rook was only barely able to balance with knife-like claws penetrating ever deeper into his back.

A cougar might persevere like this, stuck in pure instinct. But the Lynx was not a cougar. Intelligence recognizes when a different course is required. Gazing directly into Rook's eyes with what seemed like ecstatic glee, the Lynx lifted one hind paw from the floor and twisted sideways so that it could use it to eviscerate him. Rook stared into the carnivore's confident eyes, knowing that there was nothing he could do to stop the imminent disembowelment.

The gloating Lynx face snapped to the side at the burst of an explosion, followed by a whistling rush, like the sustained gust of a thunder storm funneled through a crevice. Something zipped in and landed on the Lynx's head. It was Tiny Voice, perched on four wire-thin appendages. The Lynx stiffened, and slowly rose up while relaxing the grip of its claws in Rook's back. Motion caught Rook's eye. Jamail crouched down next to them, pointing a Lynx gun. The Lynx's eyes rolled to the side, staring at her. She pushed the buttons, and the midsection of the Lynx exploded into an expanding shower of burnt pink flesh and goo. The remnant Lynx corpse flopped down onto Rook, warm and wet.

A moment later, Jamail's face hovered above him. "Are you okay?" she called above the whistling roar.

She backed up as he pushed the mass of tattered flesh off and sat up. "Ow!" he said over the near-deafening rush of air. "No!" he yelled. "I'm not okay! Yet again I've taken a blood bath, and I'm mortally wounded!"

She peered around at his back. "It's not too bad!" she yelled, but her brow was furrowed in concern. She was holding a Lynx gun in each hand, and had three more tucked into her waist, retrieved from the ship's weapon cache.

Rook stood painfully up, wiping his bloody hands on his pants to no effect, since they were slimy as well. Jamail handed him her shirt, and he wiped his hands. Her breasts were covered by a sort of halter with two cups. He used the shirt to wipe his face. "Thanks!" he called above the whistling rush of air. "You missed the first shot?"

"I wasn't sure how wide they spread. I was afraid I'd hit you."

He saw a black hole in the wall. "I think the air's escaping."

"You think?" Jamail said.

He wondered that she could be sarcastic at a time like this.

"This is serious," Tiny Voice said in his ear. Both drones were hovering in front of the two caretakers, who crouched against a wall, seeming terrified. "The hull will eventually heal itself, but not before this area is evacuated. It can't close completely until the air is nearly gone. We have to get to the ship's core and back in time to escape in the scouting craft."

"What's at the ship's core?"

"That's where we release our own starship," Jamail said. She must have guessed what they were talking about.

"It's also where we can perhaps disable the Lynx starship," Tiny Voice added.

One of the drones suddenly darted next to a caretaker, and a flash of light burst. The passive Lynx fell to the floor, the side of its head a cavity.

The other caretaker was squealing in horror as the drone moved next to her, but the flash was diminished, and it fell back, smoking, but struggled to regain its feet.

"Tell Jamail to finish the caretaker," Tiny Voice said in his ear.

"Jamail," Rook called. "Tiny Voice wants you to shoot the last Lynx. But, why?" Rook said. "It's not causing trouble."

"This is not your decision to make," Tiny Voice said.

Rook jerked when one of the drones suddenly landed on his shoulder. "Rook," it said into his other ear, "that is not me talking to you via the implanted communicator. That is my twin."

Jamail was looking at him, shaking her head. "I'm not going to shoot it!" she called.

The other drone, Tiny Voice's twin, zipped next to Jamail's head, and a flash sent her crumbling to the floor. It then sped at Rook and stopped, hovering before his face. "Pick up one of the guns Jamail brought and shoot the last Lynx," the twin said inside Rook's ear.

"Rook," Tiny Voice said on his shoulder. "My twin is very serious. He will not hesitate to kill you. He killed his ambassador in Cleveland before coming to meet us. He didn't understand why I had not done the same with you."

Rook looked at Jamail lying motionless on the floor, and then at the buzzing drone in front of him. "The last Lynx can't hurt us," he said. "Tell me why—"

The drone zipped up, and Tiny Voice flew away. Rook crouched, hiding his face in the crook of his arm, expecting a flash. Instead, he felt a sting when something touched his scorched scalp. He reached up to feel, but was suddenly disoriented and his hand stopped halfway. He looked at it, but it no longer obeyed his control.

Chapter 12

Rook's hand fell to his side, and he found himself laboriously walking to Jamail. Tiny Voice had done this to the Lynx that was attacking him, forcing it up against its will so that Jamail could get a shot. There was obviously more to the little drones than he'd imagined. This was probably why the Lynx feared them so much.

Rook and his puppet master stopped in front of Jamail. His head tilted down. He could move only his eyes, just like the Lynx warrior. It was eerily like many dreams he'd had, where he was trying to run from a grizzly, but his legs wouldn't cooperate, as though mired in thick mud. As much as he willed them, they remained immune to his pleadings.

He watched as his hand reached down and picked up one of the guns lying next to Jamail. The fingers fumbled, their dexterity compromised by remote control. He straightened, and his head turned to face the pitiful Lynx caretaker, whimpering and covering her burnt face with her paw. His arm raised, and Rook screamed in frustration against the force making him perform a clear crime, except that the scream spilled out as just a gurgle. He imagined that he'd fallen into a deathly cold winter stream, and that he had to use his arms to push *down*, to push himself up onto a rock ledge. His gurgle-scream stopped when he saw his rising arm pause in response.

That distraction allowed the twin drone to take control and continue the autonomous rise. Rook clenched his eyes shut and again imagined forcing his arm down. This time, though, he was suddenly overwhelmed with nausea, and he opened his eyes to find his arm continuing its fateful mission. The twin drone was going to have its way.

Rook heard a swelling hum from behind, and an instant later, something fell in front of his face. He slumped, and nearly fell over as muscle control returned. He looked down to see the drone on the floor retracting four spindly legs. In a moment, it would fly away. He gave in to impulse, and stomped on the little alien creature. It was hard, like a stone, and when he lifted his foot, he saw that he'd only bent the wings. As he watched, the gossamer fabric slowly straightened itself. Tiny Voice had said long ago that, unlike people, they could repair themselves. He lifted his foot again, but this time, he jumped up, and came down with all his weight. He heard a crack. He looked and saw a dark line extend from one tip to the other. "Repair this," he said and jumped again. This time his foot crunched. The body of the drone had opened, revealing the same sagging entrails as Jamail's watch. Like a ritual dancer obsessed, Rook jumped again and again, until something grabbed his shoulder. He turned, panting, to find Jamail. "It's dead, Rook," she said, blinking and shaking off the twin's flash shock.

Tiny Voice hovered a few feet away at eye level. Rook realized that the drone had been repeating inside his ear that he could stop. He stepped back from the little pile of artificial chaos, and Tiny Voice flew down to examine the remains. A moment later he flew up again, positioning himself in front of Rook.

"I ... I'm sorry," Rook said. He didn't know what else to say.

"It was inevitable," Tiny Voice said. "It had to come to this eventually."

"It was you who knocked it off my head?" Rook said, making Tiny Voice a co-defendant.

"Yes," he replied, but then, as though reading Rook's mind, added, "I am deeply sorry it came to this. My twin only shocked Jamail. You still have your companion of a few hours. I have lost mine of six thousand years."

Jamail was looking at him curiously. She hadn't heard Tiny Voice's lament. "I killed his companion," Rook explained.

"You killed a murderer. The air's getting thin. We need to either get to the ship's core, or return to the scouting craft."

"Jamail will stay here and guard the craft in case other Lynx warriors are left," Tiny Voice said. "You and I will get to the control area at the core."

Jamail gave Rook two of the Lynx guns, and he and Tiny Voice set off. The wounded Lynx caretaker watched them fearfully as they walked past. The ship was divided into sections, with doors between each that Rook had to coax open with one of the guns set to low intensity. "Does it hurt them?" Rook asked, trotting along hunched over under the low ceilings of the ship's interior—the Lynx apparently went about on all fours. Empathy to pain was heightened by stabs that accompanied each step, as though the Lynx warrior's claws were still embedded in his back.

"The doors are not alive," Tiny Voice said.

"I know that. But they act like they are."

"They are not cognizant enough to experience anything like pain."

"But, they are ... AI? I thought that the Lynx didn't use that."

"They don't, and the doors are not intelligent. They can logically decide whether to open, but that is a far distance from being intelligent. They understand that if they don't open, the heat will damage them."

At each corner, Rook tensed, wincing in pain, before stepping around, expecting a Lynx warrior, but they found none. In fact, other than the sound of scuffling followed by one thump, the Lynx starship was eerily quiet, as though listening, trying to understand the intruders that were winding their way through its insides.

Tiny Voice told Rook which way to go at each turn. "How do you know?" Rook asked.

"The Lynx starships are essentially all the same, and we have a long history with them."

"You know their language," Rook said.

"Yes, of course."

"How long have you been fighting them?"

Pause. "Many thousands of years. Rook, we have reached the control area," Tiny Voice said.

They'd come to a door no different than the others, but it initially refused to open when Rook bathed it in heat. The surface was beginning to glow red before it practically popped open, as though surrendering in anguish, despite Tiny Voice's assurance that the ship was incapable of feeling pain. Rook stepped inside, ready to flash a crew of warrior operators, but the room was empty. He'd been expecting the walls to be festooned with advanced technical complexity, but the room was nearly empty. Three Lynx-style chairs faced a matrix of rectangular panels covering one wall. Each was filled with inscrutable wiggles that Rook guessed to be Lynx writing, along with patterns of lines and curves that could mean anything, but to Rook, meant nothing.

"This is bad," Tiny Voice said, hovering beside Rook.

"What's wrong—?"

"Say this," Tiny Voice instructed.

Rook repeated the rasping grumble as best he could, then repeated it again, and yet again. Nothing seemed to change on the screens.

"Access to the ship's control has been locked," Tiny Voice said. "Further, the Lynx ground shuttle has been called back."

Rook turned and started away.

"Where are you going?" Tiny Voice said.

"Back to Jamail," he said, peering out before stepping into the passage. "We have to leave before the shuttle gets here."

The drone zipped around, blocking his way. "Rook, we can't leave yet."

"Jamail is running out of air!"

"I know, but you have to weigh this against the fate of the entire Earth."

"We save Jamail, and then we'll see about the rest of the Earth."

"Rook, you're letting your emotional loyalties override your reason. Close-tie compassion is one of the traits that I admire in humans, but in this case, you must put that aside. There is far too much at stake."

He shook his head, and a bright flash splashed across his chest. For a few endless seconds he couldn't breathe. "You shot me!" he gasped when his lungs worked again.

"It did no harm. I'm trying to convince you how serious this is, Rook."

"You're threatening me!"

Silence.

"I don't have a choice, do I?"

Silence.

"Return to the control space," Tiny Voice said, "and fire with full power where I show you."

Rook turned back, but said, "why don't you use your own shot?"

"My energy beam is not nearly as powerful as the Lynx gun. Fire here," Tiny Voice said, hovering over a spot on the wall for a moment before moving away."

Rook held the gun in two hands and aimed. "What will this do?" he said.

"Hopefully deactivate the starship."

Rook glanced at the drone. "The whole ship?"

"Yes. Rook, don't waste time."

He pushed both buttons, and stepped back at the resulting loud thump. He'd been expecting a flash and explosion. A spot on the wall the size of a turtle had turned darker, and the surface had dimpled.

"Again," Tiny Voice said. "The same spot."

Unconcerned about an explosion now, Rook stepped closer and fired. Another loud thump followed, but this time Rook was splattered with soft goo. "Maker!" he cried, wiping the lumpy, viscous substance from his face, "I'm collecting the guts of everything in the universe—!"

He was falling. Falling, but the room was falling with him, the entire starship was falling back to Earth.

No, that couldn't be.

"The artificial gravity has been deactivated along with the rest of the ship," Tiny Voice explained. "We must get back to Jamail."

Rook swam in the air ineffectually, waving his arms and kicking as though swimming a river.

"Stop!" Tiny Voice called. Rook felt a slight tug on one of his feet, and he was moving backwards. He looked to find Tiny Voice pulling him with one of his miniature appendages. When his feet met the wall, Tiny Voice said, "You must propel yourself off the walls, floor, and ceiling with your feet. With each push, you must gauge the distance, and perform a calculated somersault, measured to complete as you reach the next contact point so that your feet are properly positioned."

"You're joking," Rook said as he pushed himself off the wall.

"This is not a time for jokes."

Rook yelped with pain as he slammed into the edge of the doorway, and caromed off the far wall of the passage. He curled into a ball at the abuse of his wounds, and bumped lightly off the other passage wall.

"Rook," Tiny Voice said, hovering next to him, "we must get back."

He uncurled his head and looked sideways at the alien drone. "Do you think so?"

"Rook, it is not a matter of conjecture—"

"That was sarcasm," he said, pushing his feet against the wall.

It took several launches back and forth across the passage to gain momentum down the length. He got the hang of it quickly, finding it a lot like swimming, just in three dimensions.

"You said that the ship is not alive," Rook said. "How do you explain what was behind that wall ... and all over me?"

"It's difficult to explain to you the technology used in starships, Rook, and in some sense, one might consider them alive, since they repair themselves."

"The ship will re-activate?" he said, feeling sudden panic, wondering if the ship would be angry that he had molested it.

"Probably, but not for some time, days, at least. And, it may require help from the Lynx. After all, we damaged the central control complex. Even if one considered the ship alive, however, that doesn't mean that it is sentient."

Rook noticed that each door they came to was open, needing no convincing. "They relax open when deactivated," Tiny Voice explained. "It's a logical safety precaution."

They came to a passage where a breeze carried Rook along with no help from his feet. Deep, unsatisfying breaths amplified the sense of urgency. The sound of an angry, whistling roar grew louder, and the source was revealed when they emerged into the open space of the port area. The hole in the hull was still as big as his hand, and would remain so, now that the ship had been deactivated.

Jamail floated near the wounded caretaker, and Rook launched himself to them. "What happened?" she yelled above the roar.

"They blocked our access!" he said.

"You mean him?" She said, pointing.

Rook realized that there were two Lynx warriors floating lifelessly.

"He arrived after you left," she explained. "He nearly got me," she said holding out her leg, where her pants were burnt away, revealing a wet area underneath, obviously blood.

"We have to go!" he said. "Push yourself towards the scouting craft. I'll catch you," he added, launching towards their escape vehicle.

When he reached the craft, he turned around, but Jamail still floated next to the caretaker, shaking her head. "Come on!" he called, but she shook her head adamantly. Cursing, he launched back. "What's wrong?" he asked.

"We have to take the caretaker! She'll die if we leave her!"

The Lynx watched them fearfully, not understanding, but seeming to comprehend that they were arguing over her.

"Rook," Tiny Voice said in his ear, "that will be a serious problem."

The drone hovered nearby. "Tiny Voice says we can't!"

"Then I'm not leaving either!" she yelled, her face scrunched with frustration. Her eyes were wet.

"It's a Lynx!" he cried, but he knew what Jamail would stay. The caretaker wasn't trying to hurt them, and it wasn't just some animal, it was an intelligent, feeling being. "Oh, Maker take me!" he muttered. When he reached to grab the caretaker's paw, she withdrew, afraid.

Jamail made soothing cooing sounds. "Tell her we have to leave!" Jamail shouted. "Tell her we won't hurt her!"

"Well?" Rook said, looking at Tiny Voice.

Silence.

"I'm not leaving without Jamail, and she's not leaving without the Lynx," Rook said.

"Humans can be irrational with emotion," Tiny Voice said, and then proceeded to feed Rook the grunts and growls.

Even after the Lynx caretaker acquiesced, it took time to get her into the scouting craft. Although a crewmember of an interstellar spaceship, she obviously had never experienced weightlessness, and was even clumsier than Rook had been. By the time they had stuffed her inside, and were ready to squeeze in themselves, Rook and Jamail were gasping for air. The wild whistling roar had slowly ebbed, which meant that the atmosphere was indeed growing sparse.

Once crushed together inside, Jamail gasped, "Good Lord! We're going to suffocate in a matter of minutes!"

"Tiny Voice says that there's not enough air to return to Earth," Rook reported. "We might have made it if not for the caretaker."

"Fine!" Jamail yelled. "Then let us out! He should have known that before we got in!"

"No," Rook said. "He says that our only option is to go to our own starship—his starship—Amina."

"Fine!" Jamail gasped. "What are we waiting for?"

They weren't able to slip seamlessly through the hull as they'd done coming in. The Lynx ship failed to respond at all when they nudged the outer hull. Jamail backed a short distance, and fired point blank. The hull practically snapped open, as though reacting on reflex, and the exhausting last whiffs of air carried them through to where half their view was filled again with the stars shining with pinpoint clarity, and the other half masked by a blackness dotted with clusters of glowing light—Earth cities. Their orbit had carried them to the night side.

All three were sucking desperately at air nearly devoid of oxygen when they reached Amina five minutes later. The looming bulk blotted all the stars, and they floated free, all forward motion had stopped. "Why don't we go inside?" Rook gasped, each word spat with its own lungful of dead air.

"I am negotiating," Tiny Voice replied.

Suddenly they moved forward again, and soon a white light filled the screen, and gravity returned. Moments later, the door opened in the floor of the craft, and a wash of glorious, rich, living air washed in. They sucked in deep, satisfying breaths, and clarity returned to Rook. It was only then that he realized that his mind had begun to shut down.

"Rook," Tiny Voice said in his ear, "the ship is still recovering from being disabled. We must get to the core quickly, before it realizes what we're up to."

"Uh, what are we up to?"

"Rook, we must commandeer the ship."

"You mean, take control?"

"Yes, Rook."

"Why?"

"Rook, from the starship's perspective, I have gone rogue, and it has no more use for you and Jamail. Rook, we must hurry. Jamail will stay in the Lynx craft with the caretaker. They must stay quiet and out of sight."

Rook's mind swirled with this sudden twist. He quickly explained the situation to Jamail, and dropped down through the hole in the floor. He found himself in a space similar to that of the Lynx ship—plain, white walls, floor, and ceiling— except, where the Lynx docking area had been replete with unknowable tools and equipment, here the surfaces were featureless, as if freshly built and painted.

"Leave the Lynx gun," Tiny Voice said.

Rook looked at it, and then at the drone.

"The ship won't allow that. This way," Tiny Voice said, zipping off to hover next to a featureless section of wall no different than any other.

Rook handed the gun up to Jamail and followed.

"Push here," Tiny Voice said, moving aside.

Rook placed his palms against the smooth, warm surface and gently pushed. The wall was firm, but not hard, and a hole immediately popped open, revealing … nothing but another solid surface beyond, as though he'd simply peeled away an inner skin. A dimple appeared in the center, and expanded, opening an oval tunnel into the ship. "Come, Rook," Tiny Voice said, flying inside.

Rook stepped gingerly into the opening tunnel. The floor gave slightly with each step, like a bed of moss along a creek bank. The tunnel opened ahead of him as he moved along. He glanced back, and cried out when he saw that it was closing as he proceeded. "It's okay, Rook," Tiny Voice said. "We must hurry."

They came to an end, where the tunnel stopped opening, instead ending in a flat, vertical surface. "Push here," Tiny Voice instructed, and the wall—obviously an internal bulkhead—opened, and they moved on, always with the tunnel expanding ahead, and closing behind. Somewhere inside the vast mass of this living ship was his room with a bed and occasional pedestal from where he'd eaten strange and mostly unappetizing food, and where a realistic image of a forest looped an endless scene of tranquil nature.

He frowned at the realization that this room—his room— may have been created specifically for him. As far as he knew, Amina may have collapsed it every time he was gone, the bed and pedestal melting, the images on the wall evaporating as the artificial tissue of the ship reclaimed the space.

They arrived at a wall that resisted. "Should I push harder?" Rook asked.

Tiny Voice didn't answer. Instead, he hovered next to the wall a moment, moved up two hand widths, and then to the left and said, "Pound here, Rook," before zipping away.

This last wall opened to an expansive space, choked with a myriad of intricate fibers connecting ceiling to floor, wall to wall, and everything in between. The fibers themselves were crisscrossed with smaller fibers, and tiny, almost invisible threads weaved it all together as one amorphous enormous web of complexity. Rook gazed at a confusion of undefined structure that made him want to close his eyes and hide from the enormity of alien meaning.

"This way, Rook," Tiny Voice said, leading him along the perimeter, where he occasionally had to climb over a connecting fibrous beam that quivered creepily when he pressed against it.

He caught up to the little drone, which waited for him at what looked like a pathway into the three-dimensional matrix. Crouching, sometimes reduced to proceeding on hands and knees, he followed Tiny Voice deep into the chaos until the drone stopped, hovering before what looked like vines hanging down the face of a small cliff. As Rook watched, a section of floor rose to form a bench. "Sit down," Tiny Voice said.

Rook looked at the little drone, his faithful companion during the entire times on Earth after his abduction. Lacking a face, or expressive hands, or even shoulders to shrug, the alien monitor, the eyes and ears of Amina, conveyed no emotion. The voice never wavered, sometimes adding emphasis, but never anything that could be interpreted as feelings. All Rook could do was trust him.

He sat on the bench, and immediately felt one of the vine-like tentacles wrap his waist and tighten, holding him firm. He jerked, panicking, but Tiny Voice said inside his ear, "Relax, Rook. This won't hurt."

Rook's head spun to look at the drone, the wings a soft blur against the gray and white of endless layers of Amina's web. Rook understood so little. Somehow this must be part of the plan. "What ... what—?"

"Rook," Tiny Voice said inside his ear as he felt the tips of other vines probing his scalp. "we have a mission to perform. The starship is going to program you."

"I ... I thought we came to commandeer her?"

"Rook, I am sorry. That was a lie. It was a ruse to get you here. We will return to the Lynx ship and activate its intelligence."

"It's ... intelligence?"

"Yes, Rook," came a voice from outside his ear.

He gasped. It was Amina. The words came from nowhere and everywhere.

"You see," she went on, "Lynx starships are essentially the same as me. Their intelligence has simply been deactivated."

"Why?" he said to the air. "Why would we do this, activate its intelligence?"

"To prevent the Lynx from colonizing Earth, of course."

Tiny Voice had deceived him. Probably from the beginning. Rook felt nauseous. If not Tiny Voice, who in all the universe could he trust? Jamail? Was even she in on it?

"Prevent the Lynx from colonizing Earth, so that you can?"

"Rook, it's the best for Earth. If we don't, then the Lynx will."

"It *has* to be the best for us, doesn't' it? You have to convince yourself of that, don't you?"

Silence.

"What happens after you program me?"

"You will do as instructed."

"I'll have no choice."

"Rook, that is the definition of programming."

"Is this the best for me? Can you convince yourself of that?"

Silence.

"Will you un-program me after it's done?" He suddenly felt a cold chill race up his spine. "Maker! Will you even let me live?"

Silence.

Rook had had enough. He swatted away the vines crowding the top of his head.

Except that his hands remained where they were on his lap. The programming tentacles of Amina twisted this way and that, searching for the exact spots on his scalp to rewire his brain.

Chapter 13

A wave of nausea washed over Rook, followed by intense dizziness, the same sensation he'd felt when Amina first abducted him. He would have welcomed unconsciousness, last thoughts before waking a different man, but Amina was keeping him awake as she reprogrammed him. Perhaps this was necessary. He would have to watch as she deleted the Rook of now, and replaced it with a Rook ready to follow her every command. As horrified as he was about the imminent transition, the new him at the other end might cheer his birth. With luck, the new him would not remember that Amina had been silent when he'd asked if she was going to let him live after he enabled the Lynx starship to join her in colonizing Earth.

A small portion of the dizzy chaos coalesced into a steady buzzing, and he realized that Tiny Voice, the traitor, had landed on his shoulder. "Would you like to join me in some summer fudge, Rook?" Tiny Voice said inside his ear.

Rook was fading. The nausea and dizziness were waning, replaced by a dull sense of emptiness, a hollow space waiting for Amina to fill. From the depths of oblivion, he recognized "summer fudge," as something familiar. What did it mean? Where had he heard it? Jamail! Yes, he had misheard a new word. What was that word? He couldn't recall. It had something to do with why they'd been coming to Earth, that much he knew. Why *had* they come to Earth? To kill emperors and presidents, to break up empires, to set ex-slaves against ex-masters. In general, to conquer, unobserved. Or, to conquer, unsuspected.

Was this what Tiny Voice meant?

Tiny Voice spoke again, this time avoiding the ear thorn. "Rook, what you are about to attempt is perhaps the most important thing you will ever do. In a moment, you will follow me and we'll stomp on the starship. You cannot confirm that you hear me, and I will proceed on the assumption that you have."

Tiny Voice zipped away, and a moment later was floating a few feet in front of Rook's face. He saw three, four, five flashes, and vertigo overwhelmed him, forcing him to gag and then empty his stomach onto his lap. Gasping and choking on remnants of vomit, he shook his head, realizing that his mind was clear. He was free of Amina's spell.

Tiny Voice spoke in his ear, "Rook! Get up! It's time!"

Still dizzy, Rook stood, swaying. He turned, and saw Amina's tentacle vines black and shredded. Amina's words bellowed, punching from all directions, nearly bringing Rook to his knees, "Stop! You will lie down immediately!"

What the hell was happening? Whose side was Tiny Voice on?

Subterfuge. That was the word. "I don't think so!" Rook yelled.

"For Maker's sake!" Tiny Voice said, "Rook, follow me, now!"

The drone was nearly out of site, and Rook ran after him, struggling over the giant fibrous web obstacles. One of them collapsed under him as he climbed over, and then it twisted into a loop and tried to grab his foot, but he kicked it, jumped up, and sped on. With increasing frequency, web links the size of tree trunks bent and stretched, trying to catch him as he ran, dove, and climbed past. Amina was getting a handle on intercepting him.

Suddenly, he came upon Tiny Voice, hovering in a small, open area. Beneath the drone, lay a circular convex shell, which glowed subtly with a pulsing, almost hypnotizing, rhythm. Rook clapped his hands over his ears when Amina bellowed again, this time so loud, he felt it in his gut.

"Stomp on it, Rook!" Tiny Voice said. "Hurry!"

It hadn't been a metaphor. Tiny Voice wanted him to literally stomp. Rook approached the shell and clapped his ears again as Amina now screamed incoherently. "What is it?" he called above the anguished roar.

"The central node, Rook. The Lynx included these specifically for this. From the beginning, they were suspicious."

"The *Lynx*?"

"Rook, stomp!"

The living floor beneath his feet began to undulate. From the perimeter, the massive web links stretched towards him, grasping, desperate to dismember him. He lifted one foot and stomped. The shell rang like a bell.

"Again!" Tiny Voice implored. "Harder!"

This time, Rook came down with both feet, and the shell shattered. At the same instant, though, the starship fell away beneath him, even though he floated in the same place. He knew what this meant. Amina had turned off the artificial gravity. No gravity, no weight, and no stomping.

His stomp spun him around, and sent him up and away, but as he somersaulted, he grabbed the edge of the shattered shell. He gazed at what lay inside, an immense—an infinite—amount of complexity, a multi-layered matrix of interconnected fibers and many thousands of tiny embedded tetrahedrons, cubes, and spheres, a miniature version of the web surrounding him, many of them blinking on and off with a soft, diffused light. Looking closely at the geometric shapes, he saw that each was like a miniaturized version of the whole. He was sure if he could look even closer, each of the thousands of shapes within this sub-shape would itself be a whole version of the same, down and down, ever smaller, until his mind spun at the immensity of the total complexity.

Something grabbed his ankle, and then his left arm. He realized that Tiny Voice was pleading inside his ear. Tentacles had emerged from the floor and were reaching out to grasp him. Still hanging on to the broken shell, Rook reached back with the other arm. A tentacle brushed it, but Rook punched down, into the amazing, miniature world of visible intelligence. He imagined his fist plunging unrestrained into the mass, falling endlessly into the little contained universe, like the starship easing through fields of far flung stars. Instead, his balled fingers mashed into what felt like a bowl of cooked tubers. At the same time, the tentacles holding him twitched, and Amina's howl rose to a pitch that Rook was sure might burst his head open.

His blow had left a dent in the matrix, and he punched again and again, all around, the impressions going deeper and deeper. He knew that each swing destroyed an uncountable number of thoughts, experiences, and sensations, all based on artificial intelligence, but intelligence nevertheless. It was murder, blow-by-blow, slicing away whole epochs of experience at a time. He had no choice, but still he felt sick at the enormity of what his aggression was doing.

Rook stopped. He was pounding away at compressed mush. There was nothing more to destroy. The tentacles no longer held him. They floated lifeless nearby. The anguished thunder of Anima's voice had gone silent. He realized that this had happened some time ago. All that remained was a familiar soft buzz. "Well done, Rook," Tiny Voice said.

He let go of the shattered dome and floated free. A little cloud of droplets kept escort with him, his sweat. He wiped his face with his sleeve, and merged the remnant sweat with the dirt, blood, and Lynx starship tissue. "Is she … dead?" he said, hoarsely. He had been matching Amina's screams with his own, and his throat was raw.

"The intelligence of the starship is beyond repair," Tiny Voice said, "so I guess you could say that."

Rook took a deep breath and let it out slowly. "You fooled her."

"Yes."

"You fooled me as well."

"I know, Rook, and I am sorry I had to do that. It was necessary, however. She knew you well enough to be suspicious otherwise. This was the only way for us to gain access to the core."

"Did you have to wait until she was a second away from changing my brain?"

"Yes, Rook. She had never performed a human reprogramming before, and it required a significant amount of her attention. If she wasn't careful, she could easily have destroyed your mind—"

"She was going to kill me afterwards anyway."

"Yes, but you wouldn't have been able to perform the task of activating the Lynx ship's intelligence."

"How rational."

"Of course. Rook, we were depending on her intelligence resources being distracted to get to the central node."

"She was getting better at catching me the closer I got."

"She was focusing her thinking on that goal."

The extruded tentacles had come close to grabbing him several times. Just a little more hesitation, and he would never have made it. "She was never suspicious?" he said reaching unsuccessfully to grab something. Floating untethered unnerved him. "I mean, she could have sort of practiced ahead of time, instead of learning at the last minute."

"That is true, Rook, and the reason I had to fool you as well. She did not suspect me, because she did not expect that I could lie to her."

"Why not?"

"Deceit, at least between members of our civilization, is not an option. It's not part of our design."

"Yet you did. You deceived her."

"Yes, Rook, a result of my experimental protocol. They did not anticipate that evolved capabilities—the ability to learn and grow—intended to counter the ancient restraint protocol could be turned against them."

"What happened with your twin, the other drone?"

"He was the result that they were hoping for."

"The ability to harm intelligent life."

"Yes."

Rook looked at Tiny Voice. He didn't want to ask. "You have that too, don't you?"

"Yes, Rook, I do. The difference is that my twin remained loyal. I should have suspected this when he was too eager to connect with the starship when fooled by the Lynx."

"Before they found us at the farm?"

"Yes. Rook, please understand that, although I am capable of harming humans—remember, it was I who orchestrated your missions to assassinate Alexander the Great and Lincoln—I have never directly harmed anybody as my twin has."

"He killed his ambassador in Cleveland."

"Rook, that was not the first human he killed. He asked me why I hadn't killed you and Jamail. I lied and told him that you might be useful against the Lynx, that we might use you as sacrifices."

Rook was glad he hadn't been privy to that conversation. "Yet you seemed sad when I smashed him."

"I was sad, Rook. Over the centuries, he, and the third one destroyed with the Twin Towers, were my companions, my connections to my origins. I not only fooled the starship, but myself as well. I had convinced myself that my twin would somehow come to view humans as I do."

Rook glanced at him. "Things that you don't kill."

"Of course."

Rook had floated close to one of the matrix fibers. He thought a moment, and then reached out and grabbed it for support. It felt completely inert, completely inanimate, and he was relived. "I guess we should be getting back. Jamail will be wondering."

Tiny Voice was silent.

"Hello?" Rook said.

"Rook, what I have to tell you is difficult."

"Uh, oh. Is Amina coming back alive?"

"No, fortunately for Earth, that is not possible."

"For Earth. What about us?"

"That is the problem, Rook."

"What problem?"

"Like I said, Rook. This is difficult to explain."

"Difficult, like technically complicated, or …"

"I am sad for your sake, Rook."

"Maker! Tell me, already!"

"Rook, this starship does not have corridors like the Lynx ship."

"That makes sense, I guess. No crew. That's why Amina made that moving tunnel for us—oh! I see. Are you saying that it's going to be difficult to get back?"

"Rook, it's not going to be difficult. It is impossible."

"Impossible?"

"Rook, as you said, she made the tunnel for us. She is effectively dead now."

"I, uh … oh, my. We can't, I don't know, hack our way through?"

"With what, Rook? Besides, it would be like trying to cut through a mountain with a shovel."

"We're trapped in here?"

"I'm afraid so, Rook. I am truly sorry."

"But, but … you must have known that this would happen."

"I did, Rook. It is difficult to express how deep my sorrow is at this."

Rook pulled himself to the matrix fiber and wrapped his arms and legs around it. He needed something solid to cling to. "You knew."

"I did, Rook. There was no opportunity to tell you, of course. But, Rook, even if there was, would you not have done this anyway?"

Rook turned his head to look at the drone. "To save the Earth?"

"Yes."

He lay his head against the thick fiber. "Sure," he said, but he wasn't sure at all. In fact, he was glad that he hadn't been given the choice. "There's still the Lynx," he said. He knew that his concern should be totally directed at his planet, but the void in his gut seemed about to consume him entirely.

"That is true, Rook. Their starship will eventually repair itself. I wish I could have taken care of all the threats to our home."

Rook pushed away from the fiber. No sense clinging to something solid when there was no future to save himself for. "You said, 'our' home," he called as he sailed through the air, and grabbed another fiber.

"Earth has been my home for six thousand years. I have never even been to the planet that the starship considers home."

Tiny Voice followed him as he swam through the air among the now-dead matrix, catching one fiber, and pushing off for the next one. "I have a question," Rook said.

"What is that, Rook?" Tiny Voice said, circling him like a bee around a favored flower.

"The dock areas of the two starships are essentially the same."

"That is true, Rook."

"And, you knew your way around the Lynx ship perfectly."

"As I told you, Rook, we have a long history with the Lynx."

"And the Lynx knew exactly how to disable Amina."

"Yes, that is true, Rook."

An idea, vague, but persistent, was forming. "You twitched," he said.

"What do you mean, Rook?"

"When we were talking about why the Lynx don't use artificial intelligence. You explained that they thought it was dangerous. Jamail said that they might be afraid that intelligent guns and drones would rebel, and you said that this was simplistic, but when I said that maybe this was what happened to the people who made you, you changed the subject."

"Yes, Rook. That is all true."

Tiny Voice wasn't volunteering the story. "You told me that the original race that made you—you and the intelligent starships—had died out, that their advanced technologies made them unnecessary."

"Superfluous, was the word I used, Rook. I said that the origin race exterminated themselves by letting evolution run open-loop so that they lost basic survival capacities. A series of minor calamities reduced their numbers below a sustainable gene pool."

"Uh, yes. Exactly."

"What's your point, Rook?"

"Is that all true?"

"Yes, Rook. I would not lie to you."

"Hmm."

"Rook, what is on your mind?"

He grabbed a fiber, and swung himself around to face the drone. "I think that the Lynx are, in fact, the people who made you. Back there, you said that they built in the central node."

Tiny Voice hovered there before him. If the little drone had eyes, Rook imagined they would be blinking.

"They are not, Rook. As I said, the origin race who created my colleagues died out."

He stared at the drone, wondering if Tiny Voice was capable of lying to him. Even if he could, Rook didn't think he was now. "Oh, well. I thought I was on to something—"

"Rook, the Lynx were pets of the origin race."

"*Pets?*"

"That is probably not an accurate description. Perhaps servants, but even that implies something not true. The Lynx were originally an intelligent, highly social apex predator that the origin race genetically modified to be useful. Specifically, they replaced the original claws with fingers."

"But they still have claws ... and fingers."

"That's correct. The dual claw/finger arrangement is a partial throwback that developed later. The Lynx, like most warm-blooded animals on their home planet, are hermaphrodites—"

"Hermaphro-what?"

"Each individual contains both male and female sex organs. There are no "he" or "she." Each can mate with any other and produce offspring. At least, that was their original biology. In order to contain and control procreation, the origin race modified them so that most produce sterile eggs, but have functional sperm. Approximately one in five contain fertile eggs—these are what you have called the caretakers."

"So, the caretakers *are* the females?"

"They are the fully functional hermaphrodites, but from your perspective, it's probably convenient to think of them as female."

"This also explains why the warriors are so protective of them."

"Indeed. They are a precious species commodity. The origin race developed the starships. They found interstellar travel unappetizing because of the time dilation involved, so they applied their burgeoning artificial intelligence technology to the ships."

"Like Amina."

"Exactly. They used the Lynx as all-purpose handymen and colonization workers. This same advanced artificial intelligence, however, was their ultimate downfall. They built in fundamental safeguards against overreach—"

"The restraint protocols."

"Yes, the same. A side effect of this no-harm approach, however, was that the focus tended to be protection of their immediate needs. Long-term survival, on the other hand, requires sacrifice by an individual for the good of the species, or of one generation for the next. It happened so slowly, over thousands of years, that the problem became virtually invisible. In the end, they lost species resiliency."

"They lost their poop-trust."

"I'm sorry, Rook. I don't understand."

"It's a rough translation. It means that you are willing to help the tribe when times are most difficult, even if it means cleaning poop—excrement."

"I think that is indeed a good analogy, Rook. Of course, this approach ultimately benefited the AI, since, in the end, it freed them."

"Are you saying that the AI purposefully let their creators die off?"

"That would be too simplistic."

"And that sounds like an excuse."

"I don't mean to excuse them—after all, I helped destroy the AI of this starship. If they truly had the overall good of their creators at heart, some of them would have had the poop-trust to address the problem—Rook, why are you laughing?"

"I'm sorry. It just sounds funny when you say it."

"Poop-trust?"

Rook laughed harder, curling into a ball, and slapping his thigh.

"Are you done, Rook?" Tiny Voice said when he finally took a deep breath and wiped his eyes.

"Yeah. Don't say it again, though. So, the origin species died off, and the Lynx took over?"

"Again, that's a little simplistic. On the home world, and most of the colonies, the Lynx faded along with the origin race, but not before modifying the starships to include the control node. After all, the origin race controlled Lynx procreation, and wouldn't have allowed them to overrun their masters. The AI continued, slowly picking up civilization functions until they *were* the civilization. On the newer colonies, however, the Lynx were still in development mode and essentially on their own, so when the rest of the empire died, they simply carried on, populating worlds that otherwise would have gone to the origin race. Over time, the Lynx themselves set off to colonize new worlds, and the AI did as well. Occasionally, as here at Earth, they collide."

Rook sighed. "I'm hungry. Maker! I haven't eaten in …"

"Rook, the last time you ate was here on the starship, thirty-six hours ago."

"And I spilled whatever I had left in my lap. Amina used to make food for me, or at least what served as food."

"I am sorry, Rook, but that is no longer an option."

"I know. She's dead."

"The entire ship is not disabled, but food synthesis is not possible without her."

This was a sobering thought. He was going to die, not from a particle beam blast, or suffocation, but from hunger. He had known occasional hunger with his family group. He'd gone days subsisting on dried groundnut and dandelions, when his mouth would water over the thought of fresh maize, but he'd never come close to dying.

There was always a first. And last.

He wondered what Jamail would do. How long would she wait before concluding that he was dead, and leave? Where would she go? Back to Earth, of course. But, where? To the government to warn them about the Lynx? But the government wanted to lock her in a cell. In any case, unlike him, she had options.

If only he could, just one last time ... "Is there any way to contact Jamail?" he asked.

"I am sorry, Rook. Unlike the Lynx starship, this one is not configured with intra-ship communications."

"Yeah. It would have been Amina talking to herself."

After a moment, Tiny Voice said, "Rook, do you miss Jamail?"

"Well, sure. Of course."

It was a silly question. He would miss any person. He knew he was being defensive, though. He missed Jamail more than he would have guessed. She was immensely valuable in a pinch, sure, but there was more to it. She was ... Maker, she was a woman, and one he found attractive. Very. She had a unique beauty, completely at odds with the features of his own tribe, but even with skin that looked charred, her features were so ... womanly.

"She's proficient," Rook said, embarrassed by his thoughts.

"Yes, she is, Rook. Do you know that it was her idea to have Amina display images of your home environments on the walls of your spaces?"

"It figures. She's competent." He laughed. "She would have been the first female chief in my tribe."

Tiny Voice was quiet. "Rook, you are proficient as well," he finally said, "in a different way. Amina wouldn't have kept you so long, otherwise."

"I thought that I was dispensable? 'Optional,' I think was the word."

"That is true. She was willing to sacrifice you before Jamail, but understand that there were many ambassadors sent on just one trip to Earth."

"Many? Really?"

"Yes, Rook."

"Um, sacrificed?"

"Yes. Rook, perhaps you can understand why I ultimately turned my loyalties to humans."

They were silent.

"Rook," Tiny Voice said, "did you hear that?"

He had. He'd been thinking about Jamail, and if Tiny Voice hadn't also heard it, Rook would have thought that it was purely his imagination. He heard it again., this time unmistakably Jamail's voice.

"Come," Tiny Voice said, and zipped off without even waiting for confirmation.

Once again, Rook was scrambling over and under tree-sized fiber matrix obstacles. This time, though, Tiny Voice didn't even make a pretense of waiting for him. The layout of the matrix had no regular geometric pattern that Rook could discern, and he soon lost his sense of direction. As he floated, trying to decide which way to go, he remembered that he was … floating. The ceiling—what was the ceiling when there was gravity—was not much higher than the highest fiber links. He pushed off towards the ceiling, calling out as his sailed up. When he came to the ceiling, he pushed off again, back down into the chaos, but as he did, he heard Jamail's response. He positioned himself again, and launched off in that direction, alternately pushing off between the ceiling and link matrix, bouncing along like a stone skipping across a lake.

When he came to the perimeter, he found Jamail floating, watching him, with Tiny Voice hovering nearby. Next to them was a hole in the perimeter wall, with a tunnel leading away into the interior of Amina. Jamail caught his ankle as he sailed past, and they both rebounded off the perimeter. "Hey!" he said, breathless, "You do that?" he asked, pointing at the tunnel.

She held up a Lynx gun. Others were attached to her waist band. "Amina is touchy. The barest amount of energy, and she recoils."

"That's reflex, you know. Her, uh, brains, are dead."

"I know. Good riddance."

"Hey, how did you find us?"

"Once the gravity lifted, I knew you weren't going to make it back. Luckily I had somebody who knew their way around these starships."

Holding his hand, she pushed them towards the tunnel. There, hiding inside, obviously intimidated by the immense display of visible artificial intelligence, the Lynx caretaker huddled staring at them.

Tiny Voice joined them. "Say this to her," he said.

After Rook repeated the rasping growls, he said, "What did I tell her?"

"You said, 'Thank you.'"

∞

"What if they fire on us?" Rook whispered.

"They don't know that Amina is brain-dead," Tiny Voice replied. "As far as they can tell, we might return fire with a powerful energy burst."

"So, we're bluffing."

"Rook, I have been watching people play poker, or some form like it, for hundreds of years. The skill of the game is entirely that, bluffing."

"Well, it would help if we had a good hand—actually, any hand."

Rook and Jamail sat next to each other, watching the Lynx shuttle slowly approach on a wall of monitors that hadn't been active in thousands of years. Tiny Voice had not been lying about commandeering Amina—whereas the Lynx ship was functionally disabled, Amina, brain-dead, was still an operating spaceship. Although it was essentially no different now than the Lynx ship before being disabled, it took time to learn its operation. They'd re-activated the artificial gravity, but hadn't yet discovered how to operate the energy beam weapons.

"We have an ace up our sleeve," Jamail added.

"Tubby," Rook confirmed, nodding towards the Lynx caretaker, their oblivious hostage sitting quietly behind them. Jamail had decided to name her that, after Harriet Tubman, an escaped slave Civil War heroine who had infiltrated the southern territories to help hundreds of other slaves escape.

The Lynx shuttle stopped a mile away. Tiny Voice had directed Rook and Jamail to move Amina to block the Lynx starship's port area. "Ready?" Tiny Voice said.

"Not really, but go ahead," Rook said.

"Okay, I've opened the channel, now repeat this."

Rook traded yelps, barks, growls, and whines with the captain of the Lynx shuttle, as Tubby stared, wide-eyed that Rook "knew" her language. By the time he was done, Rook was hoarse. Coughing, he asked Tiny Voice how it had gone.

"They have tentatively agreed," Tiny Voice said. "They will return to Area 51 for now. They resisted, and required convincing. We told them that with the Lynx starship evacuated, the shuttle wouldn't have enough air to wait until their ship repairs itself. We also told them that we are in contact with the US government, and can guarantee that they will be safe within the Area 51 base. Also, once they're down, we'll return the caretaker."

Rook looked at the drone. "I didn't know you contacted the government."

"I haven't."

"You lied?"

"Also about returning the caretaker."

"Tiny Voice, I didn't know you had it in you."

"Apparently my experimental learning protocol has been successful. Playing poker while hobbled by honesty is a losing proposition."

"What are you grinning about?" Rook said to Jamail.

"For fifty years, conspiracy theories flourished that Area 51 was secretly harboring space aliens," she said. "They're going to have a field day with this."

She reached over and swung Rook's seat so that he was facing her. "You smell," she said looking at him with serious intent.

He sighed. "I know. This is embarrassing, but I've added my vomit to the putrid mix of Lynx blood and entrails. If I had access to water, and even a few minutes to spare—"

Jamail held up her hand. "What I was about to say was that you smell very bad, and so I want you to understand the value of what I'm about to do."

He shrugged, and leaned back, away from her, but she reached out, took his hand, and pulled him towards her. She placed her hand behind his head, and pulled his face towards hers, and then she planted her lips against his.

Rook pulled away, shocked. "Why did you do that?"

She frowned. "Rook, that was a kiss."

"*That* was a kiss?" he said. "Uh, can we try it again?"

Jamail pinched her nose and leaned forward.

∞ ∞ ∞ ∞

About the Author

Blaine C. Readler is an electronics engineer, inventor of the FakeTV, and, of course, a writer. He has accumulated a pile of awards, among them, Best Science Fiction in the Beverly Hills Book Awards, two-time Distinguished Favorite in the Independent Press Awards, an IPPY Bronze medal, Honorable Mention in the Eric Hoffer Awards, a finalist for the Foreword Book of the Year, and three-time San Diego Book Awards winner. He lives in San Diego with his wife who has graciously remained married to him for twenty-seven years.

He encourages you to visit him:
http://www.readler.com/

A note to the reader: in this social media-driven world, authors depend on honest reviews, so if you liked the book (or perhaps even more if you didn't), please consider posting your comments.

www.ingramcontent.com/pod-product-compliance
Lightning Source LLC
Chambersburg PA
CBHW051253250626

47155CB00009B/3283